WHEN DARKNESS FALLS

Edited By Donna Samworth

First published in Great Britian in 2016 by:

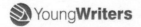

Coltsfoot Drive
Peterborough
PE2 9BF
Telephone: 01733 890066
Website: www.youngwriters.co.uk

FOREWORD

Welcome, Readers!

For our latest Young Writers' secondary school-age competition we set our writers a task: to produce a spine-chilling short story of no more than 100 words, with a beginning, middle and end.

I am delighted to present to you 'Spine-Chillers – When Darkness Falls', a collection of ingenious storytelling full of tension, suspense and atmosphere. Within this anthology you will be transported to scenes of haunted houses, forbidden forests and ghostly graveyards; occasionally finding gruesome ghouls, crazy clowns and maybe the odd vicious vampire looking for a bloody bloodbath. Your senses will certainly be on high alert with every turn of the page.

The standard of entries, as always, was extremely high and judging proved to be very difficult but I'm delighted to announce that Andromeda Gibb has been selected as the overall winner in this anthology for their spine-tingling tale. I would like to also congratulate all the talented writers featured in this collection; editing this book was a great pleasure.

Without further ado, make yourself comfy, dim down those lights and... prepare for a scare!

Donna Samworth

CONTENTS

Beth McCartney (13)	27
Ellen Johnson (13)	28
David Henderson (14)	28
Jack McFetridge (13)	29
Alison McPeake (14)	29
Dylan Robinson (13)	30
Gillian Kennedy (14)	30
Ellie Canning (12)	31
Zoe McCord (13)	31
Kirsten Peacock (12)	32
Jamie Alexander (14)	32
Sian Alexander (13)	33
Sara Galloway (14)	33
Abbie Bullick (12)	34
Rachael Stewart (14)	34
Briony Gaston (13)	35
Yvonne Grace Stone (15)	35
Bethany McClelland (13)	36
Ben Purdy (13)	36
Chloe Jamieson (13)	37
Nathaniel McCaughern (13)	37
Jude Currie (13)	38
Jack Stewart (14)	38
Jake Houston	39
Madison Taylor (14)	39
Megan Cathcart (13)	40
Sarah Fullerton (13)	40
Sarah McFetridge (13)	41
Ellie Brewster (14)	41
Abigail Morrow (13)	42
Shannyn Little (14)	42
Joshua Crawford (13)	43
Rebecca Stirling (12)	43
Oliver Jude Hampshire (13)	44
Jodie Rodgers (13)	44
Simon Penny (13)	45
Alyx Neill (13)	45
Ellen Rea (13)	46
Connor Friel (12)	46
Joel McCalmont (13)	47
Giulia Marro (13)	47
Katie Creighton (13)	48
Leah Mark (12)	48
Amy Stewart (13)	49
Julie Allen (13)	49
Katie Birrell (13)	50

Frazer McIlhagga (13)	50
Ian Logan (12)	51
Thomas Kerr (12)	51
Scott McNeilly (13)	52
Jamie Richardson (13)	52

DENE COMMUNITY SCHOOL, PETERLEE

Abbi Tuck (14)	53
Molly Lee (13)	53
Abbie Lee Nicholson (12)	54
Jake Hartley (13)	54
Jessica Hayes (12)	55
Holly Tuck (14)	55
Sophie Duggan-Crawford (11)	56
Adam Thomas Bell (14)	56
Elisha Harbertson (14)	57
Tom Brown (13)	57
Todd Lawson (13)	58
Keinan Andrew Wright (14)	58
Bethany Rose Pawley (13)	59
Kieran Newton (14)	59
Owen Rudkin (12)	60
Bobbi Chidley (13)	60
Faith Jo Inglis (12)	61
Megan Ditchburn (14)	61
Savannah Georgia Scorer (12)	62
Eden Hadden (13)	62
Nieve Mordica (11)	63
Benjamin Robinson (14)	63
Georgia Cuthbert (12)	64
Caitlin Aimee Hanner (14)	64
Regan Whittingham (12)	65
Rhiannon Pye (14)	65
Sarah Quinn (12)	66
Lucy Harris (13)	66
Demi Taylor (12)	67
Luke Williams (14)	67
Nathan Thomas Clark (13)	68
Lucy Dempster (14)	68
Ellie Walton (11)	69
Daniel Orr (13)	69
Amber Louise Travis (11)	70
Adam Grover (13)	70
Aaron Tunstall (13)	71

Brandon Gillies (13)	71
Molly Armstrong (13)	72
Nicole Rose Clarke (13)	72
Susie Ashanti Nicholson (13)	73
Nathan Tonra (12)	73
Millie Iceton (12)	74
Dominic Pearn (11)	74
Betheny Hardy (13)	75
Abbie Turnbull (12)	75
Emma Birkwood (13)	76
Luke Coxon (12)	76
David Grant Dove (13)	77
Daniel Jackson Harris (12)	77
Daniel Walters (12)	78
Paris Hunter (11)	78
Haydn Lancaster (13)	79
Jack Owens (11)	79
Abby Jones (12)	80
Nathan Sadler (11)	80
Molly Bain (13)	81
Jamie Major (13)	81
Rachel Thomas (13)	82
Jasmine Hendin (13)	82
Josh Brown (14)	83
Joseph Bentley (13)	83
Robyn Dowling (12)	84
Ben Clough (11)	84
Josh Anthony Lawler (12)	85
Savannah Justine Miles (12)	85
Jessica Paige Hardy (11)	86
Emma Hodgson (13)	86
Liam Remmer (12)	87
Dylan Mather (14)	87
Summer Louise Leigh (11)	88
Casie-Marie Porter (13)	88
Ellie Campbell (12)	89
Leah Newhouse (12)	89
Daniel Martin (12)	90
Katy Long (13)	90
Harry Masters (13)	91
Sophie Stradling (13)	91
Daniel Fletcher (13)	92
Jack Naisbett (14)	92
Ethan Howley (13)	93
Jack Walton (14)	93

DUNHURST, BEDALES PREPARATORY SCHOOL, PETERSFIELD

Ruben Alexander	94

FERNHILL SCHOOL, GLASGOW

Ella Sophie McIndoe (12)	95

IXWORTH FREE SCHOOL, IXWORTH

Jodie Manfield (14)	96
Kitty Roisin Langeland (13)	96
Brenda Louise Barrow (14)	97
Lilly Currie (13)	97
Thomas Holland (13)	98
Ellen Doyle (14)	98
Maddie Combes (13)	99
Isaac Dalglish (13)	99
Daniel James Sillett	100

KING EDWARD VI COMMUNITY COLLEGE, TOTNES

Benjamin Bilbrough (13)	101
Blake Morgan (12)	101
Jacob Finch (11)	102
Thelma French (13)	102
Kaia Lloyd-Admiral (11)	103
Verity Soley (13)	103
Karen Johnson (11)	104
Bethany Erin Ford-Hutchings (12)	104
Tegan Clark (11)	105
Summer Morris (12)	105
Lochie Poore (11)	106
Alfie Waistnidge (12)	106
Enola De Jong (12)	107
Sasha Allfrey-Jones (13)	107
Izzy Marshall (13)	108
Elliott Burrows (13)	108
Rio Creed (13)	109
Molly Campbell (12)	109

Eve Aspland (12)	110
Robin Poynter Taylder (11)	110
Benjo Aptroot (13)	111
Charlie Jones (13)	111
Maria Morley (12)	112
Alana Wells (12)	112
Rhiannon Pope (13)	113
Amélie Easton (12)	113
Lewis Corlett (13)	114
Giorgia Cornish (11)	114
Evelin Swoboda (13)	115
Brooke Toms (12)	115
Benjamin Summers (13)	116
Oliver Harris (11)	116
Jasmine Brown (11)	117
Abbi Baker (12)	117
Ciaran Finn-Looby (13)	118
Jayden Paxton (12)	118
Henry Morgan (13)	119
Harland Clark (13)	119
Amelie Norah O'Leary-Black (13)	120
Jamie Medd (13)	120
Mac Toler (13)	121
Camille Street (12)	121
Lucy Phillips (12)	122
Jonjo Hawksworth (12)	122
Lily Edmunds (12)	123
Finlay Surgeon (12)	123
Carys Trump (11)	124
Jacob Smith (12)	124
Elena Aldred (11)	125
Izzy Walton (12)	125
Isahia Chauve (11)	126
Alexander Smith (12)	126
Reece Lilley (11)	127
Joe Corbett (11)	127
Cathryn Honey (12)	128
Evie Bovey (11)	128
Poppy Payne (13)	129
Ella Miles (12)	129

QUEEN MARY'S SCHOOL, THIRSK

Martha Davies (14)	130
Angel Barton (14)	130

Sophie Emmerson (14)	131
Harriet Smith (13)	131
India Turton (13)	132
Nerissa Shutt (14)	132
Megan Marshall (14)	133
Meg Olivia Ford (13)	133

SANDWELL COMMUNITY SCHOOL - WEDNESBURY CAMPUS, WEDNESBURY

Matthew Oakley (13)	134
Harry Paddock (14)	134
Nathan Sutton (13)	135
Ashleigh Glover (14)	135
Tammem Miah (14)	136
Mia Morano (12)	136
Colhum Hellier-Campbell (12)	137
Kristian Gauntlett (13)	137

ST EDMUND ARROWSMITH CATHOLIC HIGH SCHOOL, WIGAN

Katie Rogerson (11)	138
Niamh Harrison	138
Jessica Pilkington (13)	139
Alyssa Parker	139
Shay Gaughan-Rolls (13)	140
Katie McGrath	140
Thomas Bassett (14)	141
Patrick Harrison (11)	141
Jessica Louise Lewis (14)	142
Joseph O'Connor (12)	142
Olivia Mary Pattison (14)	143
Ethan Lewis Dickson (11)	143
Emily Grimshaw-Brown	144
Thomas Ainsworth	144
Molly Elizabeth Pottage (14)	145
Alison Travis (11)	145
Megan Elizabeth Harrison (14)	146
Jack Clark	146
Gracie O'Gorman (13)	147
Abbie Lundy (12)	147
Daniel Carr (14)	148
Callum Pike (14)	148

Ben Clark   149

TAVERHAM HALL SCHOOL, NORWICH

Ethan Calvert (13)	150
Ben Read (12)	150
Jack William Barnes (12)	151
Tilly Mordaunt (12)	151
Oliver James Moore (12)	152
Ben Granville (12)	152
Maddy Lewis (12)	153
Will Woodhead (13)	153
Carys Green (12)	154
Benedict Wright (12)	154
Samuel Davies (12)	155
Alice Elizabeth Moore (13)	155
Isabel Cutts (11)	156
Louis Hart (13)	156
Ruby Vaughan-Jones (11)	157
James Duffy (13)	157
Callum Richardson (12)	158
Joshua A Field (12)	158
James Burrage (12)	159
Clara Holmes (13)	159
Hugo Dodd (12)	160
Emily Elizabeth Ringer (12)	160
Guy Hall (11)	161
Holly Turner (13)	161
Sam Crossley (12)	162
Molly George (11)	162
Alfie Edward Coop (11)	163
James Livesey (12)	163

THE STREETLY ACADEMY, SUTTON COLDFIELD

Victoria Isherwood (13)	164
Emily Witcomb (14)	164
Jodie King (14)	165
Charlotte Abby Morgan (14)	165
George Chancellor (14)	166
Courtney Wells (14)	166
Rachel Wellman (13)	167
Beatrice Emily Adams (14)	167
Skye-Ellie Thompson (13)	168

Darcai Andam-Bailey (14)	168
Rhys Carter (13)	169
Niamh Powers (14)	169
Chloe Murphy (14)	170
Chloe Marie Evans (13)	170
Jacob Nordstrom (14)	171
Daniel Hawkins (13)	171
Jack Milligan (13)	172
Mia Beasley (13)	172
Rhiannon Travers (13)	173
Daniel Joseph Holden (14)	173
Nathan Casey (13)	174
Cavan Somers (13)	174
Caitlin Williams (14)	175

TRINITY ACADEMY HALIFAX, HALIFAX

Daniel Green (12)	176

THE MINI SAGAS

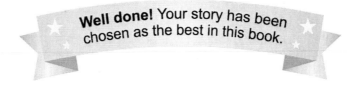

Well done! Your story has been chosen as the best in this book.

THE DARK OF THE NIGHT

He is scared. The light is on. He can see shelves of books around him. He is alone. He closes the library and turns off all the lights, except one. Not that it matters. He knew I'd be here, even if he doesn't yet know who I am. He can hear me sometimes but no one believes him. The doctors think he's crazy. He's not. I am there in the dark, he just can't see me. I am there in the light, but he doesn't realise it's me. I am his shadow, he will never escape me.

ANDROMEDA GIBB (14)
Braeview Academy, Dundee

SPINE-CHILLERS

I was alone in my house when I was awoken by an indistinct noise and reached for my flashlight. That faint tap-tapping noise was coming from across my room. Slowly, I walked across to the mirror - not daring to make a sound. I stared at it when my reflection suddenly smiled and walked out of the reflected door. I turned and was confronted my endless darkness. I could just make out the grinning face walking towards me. I stumbled back and tripped. The dark shadow leaned over as I struggled for air, I lay drenched in my own scarlet blood...

DINA HANIFAH KHAN

GONE

The creature stood before me. Abnormal with an insidious sparkle in his eye. This creature said I'd deceived his orders. I didn't mean to. He already had my soul; he'd taken everyone's soul when the world ended two years ago. Him and his descendants changed the world into dystopia and only a few of us humans survived. Frightened at what my future lay ahead, the creature took no pity. He lunged forward then swept me off my feet. My human body gone; I had been replaced. I won't be known as Rebecca, I will be known as: unidentified human species.

EVE DEVEREUX (13)

AMBER'S STORY

A girl, Amber, went to take her beloved dog for a walk. It was a dark, stormy night, and they were in a desolate forest. The dog was in a bush and Amber felt a tug on the lead. Only the collar returned. Amber was worried, she was alone, wanting to go back, but she couldn't leave her best friend behind. She kept looking. Amy was nowhere to be seen. The more she looked, the more she tired. She called Amy's name and suddenly everything went black. In front of her, Amy, lay, battered, bruised. Amy lay on Death's door.

OLIVIA BEAUMONT

Home Sweet Home

It was long ago that this place made holes in my heart. Never mind, what's done is done. I take my things and leave. Sadly, I only have until midnight.

The creaking door's so familiar. I slam it shut, I don't know why. I feel sick. I feel so uneasy. I take a seat on the couch. This all feels wrong, but it's okay, right? I have time... all the time in the world to retrieve my... What was I here for?

Never mind, it's all right to stay here. It's all right to stay at home. Right Mom? Dad?

Julian Carl Guerttman (13)
Akeley Wood Senior School, Buckingham

The Children In The Walls

I open the door to the house, wanting to access the memories of when we lived here: the evening walks, the snow...

The floor creaks, startling me. Going into the lounge, I realise nothing's been moved. I sit down, overcome with dizziness and hear a voice. 'Hello?'

Cautiously, I creep into the playroom where most of my days were spent. I look around, but cannot find the source of the voice. I lean against the wall, looking behind the cupboard, when a dusty hand grabs my neck. Just before the darkness swallows me, I hear the voice...

'I'm you.'

Guy Johnson (13)
Akeley Wood Senior School, Buckingham

TRICKS IN THE DARK

As I pounded along the faint forest track, the tangled arms of the trees beckoned to me in the night sky. I was sightless, but I knew the trees were calling. I glanced behind me and saw it gliding... A light flashed, and turning, I realised my hunter was myself: my shadow.

SOPHIA PHYLLIS LILY SMITH (14)

Akeley Wood Senior School, Buckingham

The Cobbled Path

I ambled along a cobbled path, I suddenly felt a spine-rippling chill through my back. 'Harry?' I yelled. No reply. My friend, Harry, had become lost on this path hours ago. It was dark as death. It was already night. I walked to the nearest civilised area I knew of: an old village by a rundown amusement park. After what felt like centuries I reached the park. Some light sparkled through the window of the funfair, so I decided to investigate. The door creaked open and I will never forget the horror that I saw.

Jake Dunn (12)
Bedwas High School, Caerphilly

Home

A spine-tingling shiver went through my body, making me shiver. I stood outside the Black family mansion. It had been empty for decades. The wind howled. The darkness of the night reminded me of death. I remembered the water fights in the summer, baking apple crumble, every Sunday, with Mother. I remembered planting the roses, that now stood overgrown, my marriage to my childhood sweetheart. Everything that I should have forgotten, came flooding back to me. I even remembered the birth of my first child, Martha. I remembered her first day at school, then her marriage. I was finally home.

Ella Bailey (13)
Bedwas High School, Caerphilly

THE COTTAGE

The silence of the forest was malicious. I was lost. Fog began to creep around the gnarled trees that surrounded me from each side and the rain poured down. As I stumbled around the crumbling rocks of the trees, I noticed that it was beginning to get darker. I noticed a small cottage in the distance. As I opened the creaking door I recoiled. The house smelt grotesque. The rain was getting heavier. I ventured on into the house. I froze as from beside my shoulder, 'Hello,' whispered a voice…

JESSICA OSBORNE (13)
Belfast Model School For Girls, Belfast

THE INVISI-KILLER

Snow crunched under my feet, trees swaying in the breeze. I trudged forward, lost in the gigantic, dark forest. It was late, I had walked for hours. My feet ached. Wind blew, sending several chills through me. I came to a crumbly bridge. As I approached it I heard a crunch of snow behind me. No one was there. I noticed footprints pacing towards me, but no person. I backed up instantly, *bang!* I fell and crashed onto the bridge. It crumbled and I fell into the icy river below, plunging into the darkness, sinking lifelessly down to my doom…

ALANNAH NICHOLL (13)
Belfast Model School For Girls, Belfast

REALITY

Branches clawed at my feet as I sprinted. I needed to get away. Figures seemed to grasp at my limbs, threatening to engulf me in shadows. A being materialised behind me, radiating malice and malevolence. I launched forward, avoiding her grasp. I felt betrayed as I fell. Although, I kept falling, until I awoke. Sudden and startled, I shot up from my slumber. It was a dream. Yet it felt so real... That's when I noticed her. Sickening cracks of joints popping echoed throughout the room as she rocked back and forth on her heels. She was real too.

GEORGIA ELLIOTT (15)
Belfast Model School For Girls, Belfast

THE MYSTERIOUS CASE OF THE CORPSE

The crimson-red blood splattered across the damp, gritty pavement. The limp body fell free from the rusted shackles that imprisoned it, twisted in unsettling ways. I felt faint. It all seemed so surreal. 'Huh…? You… He…' my voice trembled as my wide eyes scanned the decaying corpse. 'How… long?' I couldn't finish my sentence. As a dark, glove-covered hand clamped over my quivering mouth and muffled my terrified screams. What was happening? I didn't understand. My last thoughts faded as darkness engulfed my blurry vision.

TORI GRAY (14)
Belfast Model School For Girls, Belfast

NEEDLES

Jane lay uncomfortably in the doctor's chair. 'Will it hurt?' she asked.

The doctor bared his fake, gleaming teeth, 'A little.'

Jane started biting her nails. Her husband had suggested she should get ear surgery. 'It'll make you look prettier for me,' he had said.

'This'll numb the pain,' the doctor said before he stuck the small needle filled with a clear liquid into Jane's ear. Jane felt a sharp pain trail through her head. The doctor screamed. As the liquid filled her bloodstream, thoughts of bloody murder bounced off the walls in Jane's mind, longing to be let out.

AMY LORIMER

Braeview Academy, Dundee

MY VALENTINE'S HORROR

Finally, I was going home after a long, exhausting day of work. This Valentine's Day had been the worst, I had sat in a dull, boring office sobbing my heart out. When I reached my apartment building, I could hear whispering and footsteps in my apartment. I slowly got my key from my old bag and twisted the lock. I pushed open the squeaky door to see Danny standing in the doorway, surrounded by the rose petals and candles that framed my hallway. Danny was buried yesterday.

NICOLE BURNETT (14)

Braeview Academy, Dundee

THE TALE OF FRIDAY THE 13TH

Dear Diary, I finally got permission to investigate the most haunted place in America... Radley Asylum.

7pm - We have just arrived at Radley Asylum, we have to start setting up the cameras before it gets too dark.

8.30pm - We have just finished setting everything up, now time to split up...

9pm - I have now split from the others, they have locked me in the morgue with a night vision camera as my only source of light.

11pm - It's been two hours I think, it's hard to keep track...

12am - The room temperature has lowered. I am not alone...

NEAVE BURRY (14)

Braeview Academy, Dundee

THE LIFE OF A DEAD MAN

There are people all around me, but everything is silent. I can feel my claustrophobia coming into play. I hate this hole. I don't know how long I will be here for. I don't know how long this could go on. People come and visit me all the time, but not a word is spoken. I want to move but I am completely unable. I can't see though I know that I am surrounded by darkness. I hate this. I hate being dead. If I knew it would be this lonely, I would've burned myself alive.

NAIRN THOMSON (14)

Braeview Academy, Dundee

CROCKERY FIELDS CABIN

It was becoming night and Lily was with her friends. They decided to go to the supposedly haunted cabin that was in Crockery Fields. Once they got there it was silent. Lily heard something move behind the cabin and screeched. She said to her friends that she'd go check what it was since she scared them. She went round the corner and her heart rate got faster and faster as she got closer to the back of the cabin. She couldn't see her friends anymore. Before she could shout back, she got grabbed from behind and got dragged away.

DANYELLE STRACHAN (13)
Braeview Academy, Dundee

THE LAST RIDE

Daniel was always scared of roller coasters. Especially, when there were rumours of four boys that died on The Last Ride before the theme park closed. But it had now re-opened. Daniel was pressured by his friends to go on The Last Ride. While in line Daniel felt like something was off. Daniel's friends had gone on the ride before him, so Daniel was alone. As he sat down, he realised he was alone on the ride as well. But he felt the cold, spine-chilling presence of four ghost boys. One ghost said, 'Join us, Daniel.'

DARREN KIERAN ROBERTSON (14)
Braeview Academy, Dundee

JERRY! JERRY! JERRY!

'Good evening ladies and gentlemen, my name is Jerry Springer and welcome to the Jerry Springer Show!'
'Jerry! Jerry! Jerry!' chanted the crowd.
'Today on the Jerry Springer Show we have a mad woman who stabbed someone for cheating with her man!' exclaimed Jerry! Please welcome out Dee!' The crowd applauds. 'What brought you to my show?' asked Jerry.
'Well, I got stabbed by some crazy girl because I 'cheated' with her man,' replied Dee.
'That's horrible!'
'Let's bring out Shaniqua!'
Dee looked mortified. 'You stole my man! Now I'm gonna end your life!' Shaniqua threw her knife at Dee...

DALE SHEARER (14)
Braeview Academy, Dundee

THE MIRROR

As I woke from my deep sleep, I heard the mirror creak. I wandered over and stared at the reflection. It wasn't me. Instead, it was a black figure. I moved my arm and the figure moved too. As our hands touched the frame, the mirror disappeared. I turned round and saw it behind me. The black figure reached for my face. I realised that it was the same thing that took my sister, and I could see her staring back at me. She was the black figure now.

KIM WRIGHT (14)
Braeview Academy, Dundee

THE SCREAMS

Allison was set to take a shot of her bow when she heard blood-curdling screams. Lowering her bow and walking towards the sound, she walked for what seemed like hours hearing screams at every inch of the currently silent forest. She thought she was crazy until she saw a dark red substance. Instantly knowing what it was she followed the trail and was led into a burnt down house. She walked in, aiming her bow and saw two wolf figures fighting. She was utterly shocked to see one figure turn back into her boyfriend, before accidentally shooting at him.

CHLOE STRACHAN (14)
Braeview Academy, Dundee

NIGHTMARE IN THE FOREST

It was a dark and stormy night. Joe was walking home when he heard a shrieking sound coming from the woods. He noticed a trail of bloody footprints. He contemplated whether or not to follow them. Eventually he decided to go. He saw a body in the lake. Joe turned to run but before he could get away, a dark shadow grabbed him and launched him into the air.
He woke up in a daze, lying in mud, with his shirt ripped off and a tattoo on his chest announcing: 'One of us!'

SEAN KINDLEN (14)
Braeview Academy, Dundee

JAMES AND THE HAUNTED CASTLE

James was out camping one night with his friends and they decided to put their tents beside a haunted castle. James and his friends heard people laughing behind their backs. When they turned around there was nothing there. The weather was terrible, it was raining and the wind was like a hurricane, and their tents just about blew away. James thought he would be funny and go into the castle but as soon as he stepped into the castle, the doors locked behind him then all they heard were screams and laughs. James didn't make it out the castle.

KIEREN BARRON (13)
Braeview Academy, Dundee

THE CEMETERY

I am alone in the cemetery on this foggy Sunday. I find my sister's grave but as soon as I put the flowers down, I feel something cold go through me. I get up as it begins to rain. Then, suddenly, I see a black figure stumbling towards me. I start to walk, but the person gets faster. They are following me. I start to run. I get faster but I fall and hit my head. When I wake up, it is dark, and all I see is my sister, as she covers me with dirt, and buries me alive.

CORRIE CARVER (14)
Braeview Academy, Dundee

STRATHMARTINE HOSPITAL

As Mark and I were driving home from our friend's house we were close to Strathmartine Mental Hospital, which had been abandoned for twenty years. We stopped to take a look. As we were looking, we saw a little girl in a white nightgown. We both went in to see who she was. The floors were broken and the walls were covered in dust. In the distance we heard 'la la la'. It sounded like a child. Then, suddenly, the girl appeared in front of us. We ran out of the abandoned hospital and we never saw her ever again.

EWAN BURNETT (13)
Braeview Academy, Dundee

MOVING ON

As I opened my eyes, I saw a hooded figure at the door, scythe in hand. I knew that Death stood before me. I didn't cry, for I had no tears left. I didn't bargain, for I had nothing left to give. I took a breath of the stale, dry air and looked back at the body hanging from the ceiling. A body who had lost his wife, whose friends had deserted him, whose very existence had been meaningless. This was a body that had been condemned. A body whose owner now walked into Death's bitter embrace. Free, finally free.

ROSS DUNNE (14)
Braeview Academy, Dundee

Family Time

I put Ben in the bath with his father so I could get the washing done. I hear their laughter from down the hall. I've never heard them get along so well... Suddenly, the front door slams. I peek over the bannister to see my husband standing there. 'Honey, I'm home.' No longer do I hear the laughter.

Bobi Goring (15)
Braeview Academy, Dundee

Dirty Brother Killer

You. No. Chara stands in the end.
'Do you believe that if someone has power they must use it responsibly?' You nod.
'So then... Why'd you kill my brother?' You drop to the ground.
'I'm sorry,' you say, 'sorry you're not dead yet!' Your eyes glow red as you take your knife out of your pocket.
'Jeez kid. You sure love swinging that thing around, huh?'
The stupid skeleton fell asleep thinking I was trapped. I swing my knife.
'Did you really think it would be that easy?' I swing again. Finally dead.

Kirsten Melita Jarvis-Evans (14)
Braeview Academy, Dundee

THE CHASE

Jay turned and shouted back at us, 'Run for you lives!'
We ran as fast as we could and I stumbled down the steps of the spiral staircase and smashed my head at the bottom. My friends ran all the way home and left me there…
I woke up in a demon-looking lair with a ghostly figure. It got closer and closer and eventually jumped at me. I woke up screaming and then realised I was safe.

LEWIS MIDDLETON (14)

Braeview Academy, Dundee

MY LITTLE GIRL

This old house does not like us being here. It is a feeling I have. My little girl is upstairs sleeping. Well trying to. I hear her shrieking with horror, 'Daddy!' I stumble going up the stairs. She sounds terrified, and I am terrified for her. I ascend quickly, ignoring the gloomy and oppressive surroundings. As I enter her dark, dull-pink room, I see her sitting there with tears slowly dripping down her face, cradling the cat. Funny thing is, the cat died a while ago.

MEGAN BUIST (15)

Braeview Academy, Dundee

CREEPY HOUSE

We were walking around this creepy, abandoned house and I screamed as my friend jumped out on me. The house was dusty with broken windows and a creaking floor and rats. We got scared as this shadow came towards us and it just disappeared! I felt breathing on my neck. Next thing I knew my friend was gone and I heard a window break, she was dead. I felt something touch me. Next thing I knew, I was getting dragged across the floor.

ALANNA SMITH (14)
Braeview Academy, Dundee

BURIED ALIVE

It was a dark gloomy night, the rain battered the ground and the wind roared. Rory had found himself trapped under the ground. It was dark and really stuffy. He could hear his heart beating and his shallow breathing turned into heavy panting. It felt like someone had picked up a pillow and was suffocating him. Rory started thrashing his arms, trying to find a way out. The more he struggled, the more he became breathless. He faded into darkness.

SARAH GRAY (15)
Braeview Academy, Dundee

MAD MAN

I was running from a madman with a knife. I was trying to find my friends, I eventually found them but they were both so scared when I ran in the room. I told them, 'You don't need to be scared!' They started screaming after I told them not to be scared so I covered their mouths and whispered, 'He will find us if you keep this up.'

They pushed my hands away and screamed louder so I stabbed them and shouted, 'Shut up!' That's when I realised I was the madman all along.

JEN SINCLAIR (14)
Braeview Academy, Dundee

THE SINGING LADY

For the past few days my four-year-old son had been singing the same old nursery rhyme over and over again. I'd never sang it to him before so decided to ask him where he had heard it. He replied, 'The woman in my room sings it to me every night.'

All day it had played on my mind. I looked into his room when he was sleeping. I shrieked in horror as I heard the singing and saw a dark shadow at the end of the bed. It looked at me with its piercing black eyes...

KALLIE COUTTIE (14)
Braeview Academy, Dundee

THE ABANDONED HOUSE

My friend and I were walking through the forest on a rainy day. We came across an abandoned house so we had a look inside. We found loads of items and then we found a case full of money. After searching a little more we went over to this case to take the money and then leave but, as we picked up the case, we heard the floor creak behind us…

SEAN JORDAN CRAIG (14)
Braeview Academy, Dundee

BURIED ALIVE

I couldn't breathe. I woke up lying in a pitch-black room hearing the sound of whispering and shuffling around. I tried to scream but I just couldn't. I saw a faded light moving towards me. I sat up, the light disappeared.
I woke up in darkness. In a tiny space with little air. I shouted for help but my screams didn't seem to be going anywhere. I banged on the side of the wall. Loose gravel sprinkled on top of me. That's when I realised I had been buried alive.

ERIN COUTTIE (14)
Braeview Academy, Dundee

DEGRADATION

I've lost track of the days, the months, hell, even the years. My name was Mabel? Margery? Marcy? Something like that. I was thrown into this hellhole that I now call home. God only knows how long ago, while my sanity slowly wastes away, bit by bit. While they all sit and mock me with their murky crimson lights and their stainless white lab coats. There is a bright side though: the man in white. He gives me my gas and tablets. It suppresses the demons and makes me forget that I'm rotting from the inside out. Degrading...

BRANDON DAVID WILKINSON (14)
Braeview Academy, Dundee

THE DARK BEAST

I run through the dark forest, away from the beast. The beast that has immense, bloodstained fangs and a body covered in coarse fur. It moves quickly and swiftly in the shadows of the trees and hunts down anything that lurks through its territory. It is a killer. I search for resources. I search for food. I can only get what the forest prepares me with. It isn't much. I can only get what the beast hasn't taken already. I believe in myself. I know I can survive. I will just keep going and going...

JACK JAMES MCGRAW (14)
Braeview Academy, Dundee

THE BABY I NEVER HAD

I was woken up at around 1am to cries coming from the other room. I slowly got up and told my boyfriend, who I'm sure was still asleep, that I was going to care for the baby. I grabbed my slippers and my housecoat from the wardrobe and started walking towards the room where the cries were coming from. I got to the door, twisted the doorknob and realised, I don't have a baby...

AMY McGEE (14)
Braeview Academy, Dundee

THE STARING EYES

I enter our room in the new house. We've only been here for two weeks. My husband makes a loud snoring sound. I assume that he is sleeping so I don't turn on the light. I quietly undress. When I bend down, I feel my husband's warm breath on my neck. I slip into my side of the bed. As I close my eyes, I hear my mobile ring. When I answer, I hear my husband's deep voice talking to me. I look to the person beside me and see black eyes staring back.

ISLA SMITH (14)
Braeview Academy, Dundee

A Dead Wife With A Loving Ghost

The rain falls hard onto the old, wooden roof above me. I lie there as it slowly flows in-between the cracks and onto my chest. I hear the rain aggressively hitting the roof of our lonely house. I can't see a thing, we have no power. The wind blows through the dangerously unstable, wooden walls and through our cover. I pull my wife close to me. She hasn't moved in over a week. I hear her ghost loudly whispering in my ears at night. She tells me to keep her body close to me or I will die.

Darren Hill (14)

Braeview Academy, Dundee

The Silhouette

As I stared out my window into the torrents of rain which drenched the night-time street, I saw a dark figure in the distance. My eyes squinted to try and make out what it was. As the lightning struck, the shadowy figure had vanished. Then, as I turned around into the half-light of the room behind me, the distinct silhouette was standing right in front of me...

Erin Malcolm (14)

Braeview Academy, Dundee

THE CABIN

Bang! I sharply turned my head to see what made the noise but there was nobody there. I continued to walk through the dark, horrifying woods but with every step I got more terrified, with chills down my spine. As I walked further and further into the daunting woods, I came upon an aged, neglected, shabby cabin. The fog started to edge its way towards me. I crept up the steps onto the creaky porch, I felt the hairs on my arms stand up when I got to the broken brown door. I knocked, the door opened by itself…

CHLOE RAINEY (13)
Cambridge House Grammar School, Ballymena

THE GRAVEDIGGER

As I walked up the old, grubby, overgrown path to the historic, desolate church graveyard, I reached the rusted, rotten gate. As I entered all I saw was a land of utter desolation, old crumbling tombstone graves dug up and old human remains. I saw what looked like old packaging. I wondered why? I heard screeching and high-pitched squeals. The sound of sticks breaking made me wondered was there someone or something out there; what was it? The gate closed with a loud clang. As I walked I looked back. Oh what a horrible beast, heading straight for me!

PHILIP JAMIESON
Cambridge House Grammar School, Ballymena

THE CASTLE

Gravel scrunched softly underfoot. From the icy depths came a decrepit stone building. The only sound, a river rippling behind me. The door frame gone, carpet mouldy and decaying. Into the depths of the central hall, my torch malfunctioned. I found myself in blackness, blacker than the blackest coal cellar. I ventured forth to the Lord's tower where he mysteriously died and where his body supposedly still lies. Struck by the horror within, I ran outside into the night and, gasping for breath, ducked under a few gnarly and sparsely-leaved, tall trees and then a twig snapped behind me...

PETER STEELE (12)

Cambridge House Grammar School, Ballymena

THE HORRIFIC, HAIR-RAISING HAUNTED HOUSE

The wind howled, I pushed the rusted iron gates open. The door had been open for many years, perhaps and maybe someone was already in… The stained windows rattled vigorously from the howling wind and some were already shattered. Old paintings hung on walls, people's eyes following my every move. My face felt wet with sweat and my whole body shook violently. Splatters of dark, crimson blood surfaced the muggy, moist floor. Moonlight shone through the windows, casting a reflection on the opposite walls. A crack. The snap of a twig. Something was behind me. I was being followed: Hunted…

ELLIE ANDREW (14)

Cambridge House Grammar School, Ballymena

TINDROOMS MANSION

I crept to the gate that said 'Tindrooms Mansion'. When I opened the gate I heard a screech and there were bats but they didn't hit me. Then I heard, 'No one dares enter,' and it was a ghost. Suddenly, there was a thud, it was the gate collapsing.
'Who are you?' No answer. I started to slowly walk to the door. I was about to open the door but it burst open and I flew back and hit the ground with a thud.
He came back with a voice like thunder and said, 'Enter my house if you dare...'

JOEL BROWN (12)
Cambridge House Grammar School, Ballymena

MR SINISTER

A sudden strong, dark gust of wind wove its way through George. George was alone in the sinister, gloomy park or was he? George cautiously ambled his way to the gate. A sudden malevolent force banged it shut. He started to sweat vigorously with fright. Suddenly, a dark, menacing figure slowly sauntered towards him getting closer, closer and closer... The eerie, long screeches of the rusty swings rang through the horrendous atmosphere. George, overwhelmed, had nowhere to run. The sinister figure pulled out his axe. George's eyes grew wide and petrified. George's deafening shriek rang out. Gruesome, gory blood...

SABRINA CHAN (14)
Cambridge House Grammar School, Ballymena

AFTER SCHOOL

As I came close to the school my heart started to race. I felt like I was going to be sick. I was thinking to myself, *Has anyone ever been this scared?* The inside was as dark as stormy rain clouds. The school was freezing cold, damp and smelt foul. I walked down a hallway when I heard a child giggle. I kept hearing the words: 'I'm lost' over and over. 'I'm lost, I'm lost, I'm lost.' As I turned around I saw a child down the end of the corridor. As I blinked, looking again, the child had disappeared...

ALEX HILL (13)

Cambridge House Grammar School, Ballymena

A NIGHT TO REMEMBER...

It was a sinister, ghostly, fearsome night... We thought that exploring around the dishevelled, derelict house wouldn't do anyone any harm. Would it? The low-laying clouds wove their way in and out the ancient, lofty chimney pots. We were all shaking uncontrollably, wondering whether we should go into the house or not. The wind was blowing like a whistle, all of a sudden the rickety doors blast open and a maleficent creature awaited at the door in front of us. It was as black as coal, with two red flaming eyes. This will be a night to remember!

BETH MCCARTNEY (13)

Cambridge House Grammar School, Ballymena

THE KILLER'S CASTLE

As I crept into the dingy dungeons, *bang!* The grimy gate slammed shut behind me. There was something scuttling around, what was it? 'Hello?' No answer. I staggered on until I saw scraggly, crooked chains. There was a note saying: 'Turn back now or you might never be seen again'. My heart throbbed as I jolted forward; I could hear the sound of footsteps getting louder and louder. A shadow became visible. I didn't know what was happening. I felt threatened. I shouted, 'Don't harm me, I will leave.' No reply. The footsteps stopped and it stood right before me...

ELLEN JOHNSON (13)

Cambridge House Grammar School, Ballymena

HAUNTING HANDS

Doors were creaking. Light had vanished. I saw a flicker in the distance! As I drew nearer, the light went out. 'Hello?' Everything fell silent. Everywhere I looked was pitch-black. What would I do? I could hear fidgeting in a nearby desolate classroom. I edged slowly down the corridor. All went quiet! With the wind howling outside, I could hear the light bulb swinging in the draught, blowing through the old, rotten, wooden frames. Suddenly, my eyes were covered by two cold hands. I froze. Were they hands?

DAVID HENDERSON (14)

Cambridge House Grammar School, Ballymena

THE FACTORY

I was strolling down a rugged road on a gloomy autumn night when it started to downpour. I saw a large red sign saying: *Do Not Enter,* but there was nothing else near so I decided to go to call my dad to come and get me. When I got into the old, rundown, creepy-looking factory, the lights started to flicker and then went out altogether. I heard the sound of an old saw cutting through wood then a door behind me creaked open. I shouted, 'Hello?' but there was no reply...

JACK MCFETRIDGE (13)
Cambridge House Grammar School, Ballymena

SHADOWS AT THE SEASIDE

It was a blustery, bitter night, the sea was crashing against the rocks. The lighthouse was burning bright, I could see everything for miles. Suddenly, everything went black. I could hear thundering footsteps coming from behind. The light flicked on and off. I turned around to see a huge, horrifying, spooky shadow standing before me. My heart was pounding. I could hardly breathe. My whole body was shaking! It started rushing towards me. I bolted as fast as I could but there was nowhere to hide, I was trapped…

ALISON MCPEAKE (14)
Cambridge House Grammar School, Ballymena

THE MYSTERIOUS BARN

Cold air whirling on my face, as I walked into the abandoned barn. I could smell the rot of dead animals that made me feel sick. The fog was slowly fading as I entered and all I saw was a pitch-black barn, *bang!* 'Who's there?' No one answered. I heard footsteps above me, I realised I was not here alone. I reached for my torch, it was out of batteries. I leapt behind a box as I heard creaky footsteps coming down the stairs. I heard a loud, deep laugh. I turned round and saw a weird figure. *Boom!*

DYLAN ROBINSON (13)

Cambridge House Grammar School, Ballymena

FOOTSTEPS

It was a cold, dark, bleak Halloween night. I knocked on the old, dingy mansion door, it creaked open. It was pitch-black inside, the moonlight shone through every crack and the fog slithered in like a snake. Nobody had lived here for centuries, I heard frightful footsteps but where could they be coming from? They seemed to be coming from the wall. I leaned on the tarnished gold lamp, then unexpectedly the dull, dusty, dismal wall moved, opening a passageway! I heard the footsteps again, they were getting closer. Although nothing seemed to be there, I knew I wasn't alone…

GILLIAN KENNEDY (14)

Cambridge House Grammar School, Ballymena

THE CABIN

It was a cold, dark and foggy night. As I entered the woods I heard the loud shriek of an owl in the distant trees, I jolted forward with a fright. As I looked into the distance it was pitch-black, I couldn't see a thing so I pulled a torch out of my bag. I turned it on only to find myself at a cabin. I crept up the decaying stairs into the cabin. The door slammed shut behind me. I shouted, 'Hello?' There was no answer. I felt a cold breath on the back of my neck. 'Ghost?'

ELLIE CANNING (12)
Cambridge House Grammar School, Ballymena

RUN, RUN, RUN!

Bang! I could hear thundering footsteps. I was startled. I dashed off, I was very apprehensive and alarmed. I found myself alone in a dim, dark and deserted forest. At least, I thought I was alone. I saw a human-like figure but I couldn't make it out. I was surrounded by prodigious and dusky figures. I felt trapped. The leaves on the trees were whirling and whistling. It was a bitter night. I was forgotten and I didn't know which way was home. I shivered, I could feel numbing hands on my neck, I started to splutter and choke…

ZOE McCORD (13)
Cambridge House Grammar School, Ballymena

CHOSEN

The demented girl was standing in my room. I asked, 'Who are you?' as I speedily sprung with fear.

She told me, 'I'm Lucy, you are the one I've chosen.' I was left speechless then she told me to follow her... I did. Her face and body was gloomy grey with demonic eyes. With long raven-black hair, she took me to the dark woods whilst holding my hand with hers. There were corpses rising from graves and writing devilish words everywhere. They stood me in a circle and did a Satanic ritual. The girl then spoke... 'I chose you.'

KIRSTEN PEACOCK (12)
Cambridge House Grammar School, Ballymena

A NIGHT IN THE FOREST

Snap! 'Hello, anyone there?' I called out... The downpour drenching my clothes. I should take shelter. Creeping through the fierce forest, trees blowing, wind howling, rain pouring. I had the feeling that someone was watching me. I came to an abandoned caravan. I peered through the window. 'Hello?' I called out. No response. I went inside and turned a lantern on. I searched around for something to eat but, out of the corner of my eye, I noticed something behind a few boxes. I approached it slowly, my lantern went out. *Thump, crash.* All I could see was red eyes...

JAMIE ALEXANDER (14)
Cambridge House Grammar School, Ballymena

Psychotic Laughter

I started to regret coming here while walking through the chilling hallway of this ghastly asylum. Everyone told me to never step foot in this place for 'certain reasons'. I mean, did they really expect me not to come here? I sped up my pace now being fearful of the unknown that lurks through here. Then laughter occurred... It wasn't funny, it was almost psychotic. I started to run, faster and faster. The laughing got louder and echoed through the hallway. I then felt something sharp pierce through my leg and blood started to trickle down, then it got dark...

Sian Alexander (13)

Cambridge House Grammar School, Ballymena

The Woods

Crash! Bang! Crack! The fog was creeping in. It was already getting dark and I had taken a short cut through the weird, wintry woods. I faintly heard a vile voice shout my name. 'Mollie!' I looked around to see nobody standing, not even a silly silhouette. I started to walk frantically faster but I heard feeble footsteps steadily speeding up behind me... I found myself now spinning through the woods from this mysterious monster, when suddenly the footsteps stopped, everything was silent when I felt a cold, bleak hand touch my shoulder. I jumped and asked, 'Who are you?'

Sara Galloway (14)

Cambridge House Grammar School, Ballymena

Is This Castle Really Haunted...?

I was standing outside the unearthly building when I heard a loud thud. I went in, the heavy door slammed behind me. Then I heard a voice. 'Who is in my castle?'
I realised I was in an ancient deserted castle. A quiver rushed down my spine. I tried to go out the door but the lock was secured. I felt a bitter breeze on the back of my neck so I turned but there was nothing in sight. 'Hello? Anyone there?' I yelled. I felt a chilly hand on my shoulder. 'Help! Help!' I cried out as I collapsed...

Abbie Bullick (12)
Cambridge House Grammar School, Ballymena

The Doll In The Attic

Thump! I'm calmly climbing the ladders to the attic. *Thump!* I'm unlocking the bolt. *Thump!* There's nobody here. Where's all the deafening, thunderous clattering coming from? I hear a shuddering snicker to my right but all I can see is the dim hallway in front of me. I cautiously creep around looking for what made the horrifying sound. I see children's toys scattered around the floor and in the corner of the attic there is a sinister, ancient, clown-like doll. Is this where the laughing and thumping was coming from? The light from my flashlight flickers and, suddenly, I freeze…

Rachael Stewart (14)
Cambridge House Grammar School, Ballymena

The Ancient Abandoned Academy

As I entered and took my first step I said, 'Hello?' The door rapidly closed behind me. The lights were flickering; the thunderous wind had shattered the window opposite me. I heard a booming noise, so I decided to investigate the sound and find out what was happening. I cautiously opened the next door into complete pitch-black. I could hear that a window had been opened because I could hear the ghostly wind. I rushed to the window but it was closed! Somebody closed it on me! I turned around to see a mysterious figure standing behind me laughing...

Briony Gaston (13)
Cambridge House Grammar School, Ballymena

Bedlam

Wind is chasing up the hill, breaking through the paneless windows. Clouds of dark, gloomy filth is blown into the air. I choke, coughing and spluttering, gasping for clean air. *Crash!* I swing my head to face the noise; nothing. The screaming silence sends shivers down my spine. I cautiously creep deeper into the darkness of the dismal corridors… *Smash!* I turn to face an empty space. As I turn, I hear the mad laughter of thousands of invisible psychiatric patients. My heart pounds at a million beats a second. I begin to run but… *slam!* The door snaps closed…

Yvonne Grace Stone (15)
Cambridge House Grammar School, Ballymena

MENACING MIRTH

I hear it! I hear the cackle of it, where's it coming from? I feel my goosebumps rise, my head spinning and my heart racing... As I look around this uncanny locality my hands tremble with apprehension... *Bang!* 'Ha, ha, ha, ha! It's me!' Then silence. I protractedly creep around the funhouse. A vast shadow comes into sight. It has tresses as immense as Medusa. No matter what I cannot look at this colossus. 'Welcome to the funhouse...' it sneers. It is faceless, it has scars I have never witnessed before! Its hand drifts off its face, the ominous clown.

BETHANY MCCLELLAND (13)
Cambridge House Grammar School, Ballymena

THE MANSION

Night-time was closing in, the mansion was gloomy and creepy but it was the only place to go. I was petrified, frightened and scared but I went in anyway. I was completely lost, lost, lost. The spine-chilling graveyard surrounded this magnificent but still-creepy mansion. I crawled my way into the mansion as I heard strange noises. *Bang,* another big noise came. *Bang,* another one, I started to run and then I darted and ran as fast as I could. I kept running, sprinting, darting away from the noise. I had just felt someone touch my shoulder.

BEN PURDY (13)
Cambridge House Grammar School, Ballymena

WILL I HEAR THE ROOSTER AGAIN?

Clink! Clink! Clink! The sound of the wind rattling the chains. I gasped. I crept up to the barn, my heart pounding out of my chest. *Slash!* The storm grew near. I was lost, alone and scared. The door screeched as I pulled it open. I peered timidly into the barn, looking left and right, no living creature was in sight. I squeezed through the gap. Suddenly, a stone-cold hand wrapped itself around my neck as I fell to the floor...

CHLOE JAMIESON (13)
Cambridge House Grammar School, Ballymena

THE CASTLE OF DARKNESS

The rain was torrential and I was alone. I wandered off during a hiking trip. I was suddenly lost in a deep, dark, dense forest. There was a spire in the distance. I heard a rustle behind me so I ran. I was not alone... As I reached the castle, the doors opened. Whilst walking I saw a figure standing... staring at me. Creeped out, I started to back up. Suddenly, the figure darted at me. I woke up. It was a dream, or was it? I sat up only to see the figure reaching out for me. I blacked out...

NATHANIEL McCAUGHERN (13)
Cambridge House Grammar School, Ballymena

THE DEADLY DECISION!

It was Halloween night! I was at a haunted hospital outside town. Strangely, as I came to the entrance, it was already open! When I walked, in I saw blood on the wall and it was cold. I started to walk down a corridor. *Bang!* The door shut and I was alone in the dark. Then I caught the glimpse of a figure and it quickly ran away. I shouted, 'Who are you?'
Suddenly, I turned around and a creepy creature was less than 10 metres away from me, staring straight at me with bright, gloomy eyes...

JUDE CURRIE (13)
Cambridge House Grammar School, Ballymena

THE GUTTING

The thick fog wove in. The boys were starting to worry. The forest isn't a good place to be at night. They heard the noise of footsteps. Joe walked forward, he looked back and the others were gone. The screams of the boys echo in the forest. The withered trees cracked and bent over seemed to watch him. *Crack!* Some twigs were snapping behind him. 'Guys? Hello?' The engraving on the tree said: 'Run'. He wondered. He turned around to see a head of one of the boys that was there, hanging. He screamed. A cold hand *pulled* him away…

JACK STEWART (14)
Cambridge House Grammar School, Ballymena

WHISPERS

Rain was pouring down and I couldn't see a thing in the gloomy night. I took shelter in an old hospital while shadows and whispers haunted me. The frightful creak of opening doors around every corner and all of a sudden, a high-pitched scream echoed from corridor to corridor. 'Hello?' No answer. Everything remained voiceless apart from thin air roaming the old rusted silver chains dangling from the ceiling.

I then caught a shadowy figure that crept up on me, making each footstep loud and clear and it then whispered in an evil, wicked, deep groan, 'Leave...'

JAKE HOUSTON

Cambridge House Grammar School, Ballymena

THE TOYSHOP

The eerie shop was dark and dusty. I searched around to try and find something interesting. There was a loud crash as a frightening, spooky, scary glass doll fell from the shelf. I screamed! I tried to run out of the shop but the door was locked! I shouted then turned around, the doll was back on the shelf as if nothing had happened. I crept over to the loathsome, unsightly, bestial doll but as I turned the corner a jack-in-the-box sat in front of me, playing the most macabre, menacing song...

MADISON TAYLOR (14)

Cambridge House Grammar School, Ballymena

IS ANYONE STILL IN PRISON?

'Tours of the twisted Tellyford Prison,' announced a man with coal-black postiche. As a fellow history aficionado, I cross-questioned him where to go. The man gesticulated forward. I turned to thank him but he had dissipated. Taking no interest, I traipsed in. The place was uninhabited. I noticed a sign on the wall, it was as bright as the sun, being a neon-yellow, it read: 'Entrance to Prison!' As I infiltrated the lights started flickering. To the left was a desolate prison cell. Number thirteen... I entered. *Bang!* The door closed... I heard breathing... I plummeted to the floor...

MEGAN CATHCART (13)
Cambridge House Grammar School, Ballymena

IT ALL HAPPENED THAT NIGHT!

Bang! I just woke in a place that wasn't my home. I was lying in a dismantled bed that was infested with slug-like creatures! I screamed and heard a faint moan, then I abruptly felt a cold, dead-soul hand on my back. I froze. I couldn't move. I saw spiders crawling along the ground and fog started spiralling around me. A creepy dark corridor was ahead of me and I felt I was drawn to it. I stumbled down the hall and I noticed a tall, skinny, pale, human-like figure, but suddenly my leg... 'Help!'...

SARAH FULLERTON (13)
Cambridge House Grammar School, Ballymena

MOTHER?

As I tread through the corridors of the abandoned hospital, I can hear whimpering whispers and screams of the past patients or maybe the ones that never left? I walk into the children's wards, the painted animals on the faded blue walls had been repainted with a sparkling coat of red bloody handprints! I can't even get words out of my mouth, I am petrified. *Clank!* I turn around startled, a tray of needles fall on the tiled floor.

'Hello.' I swivel around to find a tiny girl looking up at me, in a torn dress. 'Mother?' she whispers.

SARAH MCFETRIDGE (13)

Cambridge House Grammar School, Ballymena

SINISTER FAIR

Bang! Scream! Crash! went the rides. A sudden cold chill slowly moved down my spine. I thought this would be an amazing idea, creeping into the abandoned sinister fair, on my own. Obviously not... I decided to climb aboard the rusty, decayed 'Ghost Train'. Strangely, I was curious and excited to see what was left perishing inside. I jumped into what seemed like a deathly, dark room. Cautiously, I crept in silence, trying to be as quiet as a mouse. I took one step, immediately the lights brightly struck on. My head went up and before me was my death...

ELLIE BREWSTER (14)

Cambridge House Grammar School, Ballymena

THE ROOM ABOVE MINE IS SILENCED

From the room above mine, music was playing. 'For the fourth time this week!' I grumbled and stormed upstairs. I hammered the door. 'Have some respect! Don't you know that some of us are trying to sleep?' I yelled. The music stopped, the silence became eerie, as the door opened slowly with a ghoulish groan. On the floor lay a broken guitar and a body; it wasn't moving. The dust had gathered on the floor, it was thick and undisturbed. I was shocked but delighted! Silence! Just how I like it and just how I left it last time!

ABIGAIL MORROW (13)
Cambridge House Grammar School, Ballymena

STOLEN IN THE NIGHT

It was almost nightfall and as I wandered home I came across a shortcut. I decided to follow the narrow, winding path home. The night grew colder as a thick dew settled on the fallen leaves beneath my feet. The chilling breeze blew and brushed against my cheek. I began to daydream and became oblivious to my surroundings. Suddenly, the path split into three and my head began spinning! 'Where am I?' I asked myself before sitting down on the cold, hard ground. The wind whistled violently and a huge, dark shadow neared me. Someone or something grabbed me...

SHANNYN LITTLE (14)
Cambridge House Grammar School, Ballymena

ARKHAM ASYLUM

Crash! Bang! Boom! was all I heard throughout the night. Lightning pitchforks were crashing around me! I had to retreat to a sinister, obnoxious and ominous building, it was like a penitentiary. I walked up to the metal door and suddenly it opened, it was like the house was drawing me in. I lurked in the main hall apprehensively. It had a colossal chandelier and another door. I wanted to get out as soon as possible, but something inside me made me shout, 'Hello?' The door slammed shut and I felt something drip on my shoulder, I looked up... 'Help!'

JOSHUA CRAWFORD (13)

Cambridge House Grammar School, Ballymena

THE GHOSTLY GIRL

'Is anyone there?' I asked the moonlit room. I toppled over a table that was lying on its side as I stepped through the door.
A rope hung in the centre of the room. Below it on the ground there was writing that said: 'It's your turn!'
I promenaded over to get a closer look. When I reached the writing I looked in front of me. A pale white girl stood there, staring at me. 'It's your turn!' she said with a grin. I suddenly collapsed to my knees. I looked up at her as I slowly closed my eyes.

REBECCA STIRLING (12)

Cambridge House Grammar School, Ballymena

THE DEMON'S DEN

The floor creaked and cracked every step I took on the crumbled floorboards. The colour never changed from this dull, damp grey, the same colour as the sky when a storm hit. The interior of every room was barbarically smashed up. What had happened here? The house suddenly got darker, greyer and gloomier. A strange chill crept up my back. *Bang! Bang! Bang!* The door at the top of the stairs was shaking so ferociously, I thought it had come off its hinges! I bolted like a cheetah out of that horrendous house and have never gone back since.

OLIVER JUDE HAMPSHIRE (13)

Cambridge House Grammar School, Ballymena

TICK-TOCK CHURCH CLOCK

There it was! The church that my now-dead parents got married in. I remember watching their wedding tape. I thought that I should walk in to soak up my parents' past. I walked in. I heard a faint ticking of an old and rusted grandfather clock. I wondered how could it possibly work? This place had been abandoned for over forty years. Unless someone had been in there. Everything was going through my mind there and then. As I walked further I found a pool of fresh blood. 'Hello,' some mysterious voices said. I turned around. It was them...

JODIE RODGERS (13)

Cambridge House Grammar School, Ballymena

Girl Drowns On A Fun Day Out

'Little girl drowns at Ballykeel. Charlotte Greg, aged nine, eldest daughter of Mr James Harry Greg was accidentally drowned whilst bathing in the Lockyer Creek on Friday afternoon', writes our Ballykeel correspondent.

Nearly an hour elapsed before the body was recovered. The spot, which has always been considered dangerous, is known as Murphy's Hole and it's over 20ft deep. The funeral took place on Friday 13th, a week later. The funeral was largely attended, the Ballykeel schoolchildren were dressed in white, marching next to the hearse.

'Hello? Is anyone there?' A strange voice came from the hearse. 'I'm trapped!'

Simon Penny (13)
Cambridge House Grammar School, Ballymena

The Breath On My Back...

The black car started to slow down as I began to speed up. No one was around because it was late at night. I heard the engine turn off so I ran for my life. I went into an empty shop that had been there for years. The door was open thankfully. The room was full of scary dolls. I thought, *it has to be dolls, the one thing I hate.* I heard footsteps getting closer and closer until the door opened. 'Hello?' I shouted. No reply. I felt a cold breath on my back.

Alyx Neill (13)
Cambridge House Grammar School, Ballymena

THE HANGING GIRL

Entering through my local park gates, seeing it completely destitute, the many myths of these parts make me not surprised. The hanging girl was the most famous of them all. Some affirm she still walks around, with the rope around her neck. Minutes pass and my walk has been the most undisturbed I've ever had. Approaching the lake I hear a suppressed giggle, convinced it is just in my head. As the water is so pellucid, you can't miss the chance to have a look. Gaping into the clear water the reflection proves, you were not alone... The hanging girl.

ELLEN REA (13)

Cambridge House Grammar School, Ballymena

HOLY HORRORS

In the middle of nowhere, just off to the side of the road, stood a very elderly chapel. The chapel looked as if it had just been hit by a bomb! There were shattered stained-glass windows and a very lacklustre cross towering over this assaulted building. The interior of this church was just as deteriorated as the outside of this eerie excursion. The church's rows of chairs were all snapped. Now if you wanted to go into this intimidating place of death, and wanted me to come along, no, no, no, would definitely be my answer.

CONNOR FRIEL (12)

Cambridge House Grammar School, Ballymena

The Awakening

I had been running for what felt like hours, but the concept of time had fled from me far too long ago. I searched the world around me. Everything was hidden in dense, dreary fog. *Bang!* The erupting echo could've shattered the sound barrier throughout the whole galaxy. The noise came closer, alongside a gaping shadow of a creature, replicating a human, but a mechanical cry from it proved me wrong. I continued running. The path ahead was clear until a grave, perfectly laid out for me, trapped me. No way out. The beast began my burial. Say goodbye...

Joel McCalmont (13)
Cambridge House Grammar School, Ballymena

David's Words

Gusts of wind were seeping through the graveyard, sounding like a wolf howling at the moon. *Crack, crack, crack* went the crumbling, decaying gravestones as I carefully walked over them. 'Don't disturb the dead,' David's words from earlier in the day repeated in my head. I felt as if someone was creeping behind me, every minute I turned around hoping to settle my paranoia. 'Behind you,' I heard someone whisper.
'David? David? Who's there...?'

Giulia Marro (13)
Cambridge House Grammar School, Ballymena

LAST BREATH

I walked through a relinquished hospital. Although one survivor was left. The wound had blood squirting out like a Mento added to Diet Coke. She lay paralysed and overcome by what she had just encountered. I quickly ran to her. 'Hello, can you hear me?' She never replied. Her eyes slowly closed with a smug smile on her face. A face as pale as wax, faded to death. Suddenly, a glacial pang of pain like the stab of a dagger of ice frozen from a poisoned well hit me! What exactly was behind me? I didn't really want to know...

KATIE CREIGHTON (13)
Cambridge House Grammar School, Ballymena

THE DOLL SHOP

I push the creaky door of the doll shop and immediately I see the murder scene. The place has been totally trashed. A thousand plastic faces staring at me, I'm shaking with fear now and my hands tremble as I make my way to the basement. The lights suddenly go off and the door slams behind me. I grab a nearby flashlight and continue down the stairs. That's when I see the body. How did this happen to my grandma's shop! As I start to dial 999, I'm interrupted as a cold hand slithers around my neck. I turn around...

LEAH MARK (12)
Cambridge House Grammar School, Ballymena

China Doll

Her cold, lifeless eyes are staring into mine, perfect porcelain features, without expression, hold me transfixed where I stand. 'Genuine haunted doll' was the description on eBay. I thought it was a gimmick to push up the price, but I placed a bid anyway. It arrived yesterday, it looked quite creepy. Entrancing eyes, red stained dress. I placed it onto the table and here I am. I can't move, I'm as still as a statue. I can't look away; I'm locked in this death stare. But then she inched closer and closer. Will anybody find me? Before it's too late?

Amy Stewart (13)
Cambridge House Grammar School, Ballymena

A Dancing Shadow

I was getting more scared every minute. It was dark already. The fog was growing, getting thicker every second. How will I ever get out was my main worry. The forest just seemed to continue, never-ending! I came across an old house with shattered windows and crumbling walls. My legs kept getting more tired. I needed to sit down. I crept between the trees. The spine-chilling house stood there, dilapidated and abandoned. I went in and sat on something that looked like an old cushion. A dust cloud rose. A large shadow danced across the wall. 'Hello...'

Julie Allen (13)
Cambridge House Grammar School, Ballymena

At The Top Of The Road!

At the top of the road, there stands an old, dilapidated house. The colour drained from the walls. Inside the walls are covered in crimson red blood, with old dolls covered in scraps and their dresses ripped up. Everywhere you look, no matter where you turn, they always seem to be following you with their scary glass eyes. You can always hear the laughing of young children no matter what time of the day.

Katie Birrell (13)
Cambridge House Grammar School, Ballymena

What Hides Behind Shadows

The darkness was controlling the night, every shadow that moved had a friend beside them. I was lost in the woods, campsite nowhere in sight. When would I find anything inhabited? I found a tree house. Who had been out here? I climbed the rickety old ladder. *Creak, creak!* I went inside and the tree swayed. I saw the moon shimmer through the windows. The shadow of the tree grew bigger into the shape of a human, a huge human shadow. I turned around but before I could see it I was grabbed and thrown through the forest into darkness.

Frazer McIlhagga (13)
Cambridge House Grammar School, Ballymena

THE TREES SAW!

I could hear a wolf's howl whistling through the creepy and misty forest. *Snap!* I knew I wasn't alone! Something was with me! The trees looked like they were stalking me. They were watching my every move. What was I going to do? As I walked further and further through the forest I noticed an abandoned farmhouse. Inside lay decayed, rotten, disgusting cows hanging on chains. There was also a massive hatchet covered in blood. I noticed this was a slaughtering service house. Suddenly, I started to hear heavy footsteps. I turned round...

IAN LOGAN (12)
Cambridge House Grammar School, Ballymena

THE OLD WELL

I fell down the old well. Fortunately I wasn't hurt. At the bottom there was a skeleton, a horrid thing in the tatters of a summer dress. I was terrified. I climbed out and ran to the house but I couldn't find my family, only a man and a woman I didn't know. I approached them, the man ignored me but the woman screamed, and then I realised there was something important I had forgotten. Then I was back in the dark well again, with that horrible skeleton. What had I forgotten? What was it?

THOMAS KERR (12)
Cambridge House Grammar School, Ballymena

THE ECLIPSE

The moon covered the sun. It was very dark. I could make out a few things like the cat's eyes in the middle of the road and the lamp posts at the side of the road. We stood there watching the eclipse, but the moon didn't seem to move. We watched it for about half an hour but it still didn't move. *Bang!* There was a sound that came from behind me that sounded like gunfire. Then I heard the sound of a gun reloading. Then I felt the gun pointing right at the side of my head. *Bang!*

SCOTT MCNEILLY (13)
Cambridge House Grammar School, Ballymena

THE ABNORMAL HOUSE

It was a dark and creepy night, the fog was weaving in through the houses and the moonlight created a bit of light. I was walking into an old, abandoned, rundown and vicious-looking house. I was looking for some shelter from the storm so I walked into the house and saw an abnormal figure in one of the rooms. I didn't want to experience that figure any closer. I strode towards an old sofa to sit and wait out the night, but I heard a peculiar sound and saw the shadow again. There was something at the door...

JAMIE RICHARDSON (13)
Cambridge House Grammar School, Ballymena

SHE'S COMING

I hear her. She's coming, like last night. She will tread, slowly, down the hallway. Open my door and disappear. I'm drained. A hopeless feeling is hanging in the air, it won't be shaken. It won't leave me or my daughter - she's close. I stop breathing. Small, shuffling footsteps approach my door. They stop. Right outside. It doesn't open. It carries on toward my daughter's room, the pace quickening - I hear the door creak. Then nothing. A startling scream cuts through the stillness. I try to move - I cannot. Her pitiful cries tear through the night. As I lay helpless.

ABBI TUCK (14)
Dene Community School, Peterlee

SWEET DREAMS

It started when I was six. Doctors called it sleep paralysis, said it's only a dream. Continuously, it began with sitting upright in bed, surveying my blood-soaked room, listening to violent screams ricocheting from the crimson walls. Lurking in the darkness, an ominous squid-like creature protruded sickening tentacles and emitted a deafening screech. Prickles surged through me and traumatised cries attempted to escape my unmoving mouth. With no avail, they resonated within my aching lungs. *Smash.* The dysmorphic being shattered the window, releasing my frozen body. Stirring awake, my gaze fixated on the violent, bloodthirsty creature now in reality...

MOLLY LEE (13)
Dene Community School, Peterlee

The House Of No Return

At midday, we giggled around a bush, daring Charlie to enter the derelict house. Those giggles soon turned to horror when Charlie's head thudded against the window, screaming, 'It touched my face!'
We didn't listen and we said politely, 'We will let you out in one hour!' So Charlie decided to wander around the house instead of doing nothing.
A few hours later, Mark checked his watch and it was time for him to come out. We went in. There were voices coming down the stairs. A married couple saying, 'I, 2, 3, 4, we're here!' Then they approached me...

Abbie Lee Nicholson (12)

Dene Community School, Peterlee

Truth Or Dare?

'Fine! I'll go in,' I hesitantly stuttered, as I opened the dusty, crooked, hell-like door. Cobwebs attacked my every move as I settled for a night in this haunted abode. To my surprise, the clock struck twelve with a deafening shriek. It was like the clock was warning me to leave. As deathly seconds, minutes, hours passed, it became forever frozen in time. Endless wind sent shivers down my spine. I covered myself in blankets, hoping this nightmare would disappear. But it didn't. Was there ghosts in this place? I thought to myself, *will I make it out alive?*

Jake Hartley (13)

Dene Community School, Peterlee

MERMAID MAYHEM

An underwater scene. In this evil kingdom are the shadow wolf mermaids, the most evil creatures in the ocean. The queen of the shadow wolf mermaids is Nadia. She has many servants and guards, she has two sisters, Adrianna and Oceana, however her sisters aren't evil. The shadow wolf mermaids are evil mermaids who can turn into wolves. Nadia isn't happy that her sisters aren't evil and vicious like her. The girls are trapped, there is no escape. It is haunted mayhem... Dolls' eyes are many, a girl singing nursery rhymes, blood splatters everywhere and a teddy full of blood.

JESSICA HAYES (12)
Dene Community School, Peterlee

BODIES

I grabbed my backpack then exited my worn tent. I was going cave exploring, a bit of fun, only it didn't turn out that way. I hopped down into the entrance, the golden sunrise creeping in. Bushes rustling above. It wasn't the wind. I delved further into the maze of grey walls. I turned a corner and a shockwave of terror coursed through me. Hanging from the ceiling were children's bodies - dozens of them. Then I felt a sharp blow to my head, my ears started ringing and I fell to the floor, hitting my head once more. Then nothing.

HOLLY TUCK (14)
Dene Community School, Peterlee

THE ABANDONED CHURCH

Shadows all around, suddenly I saw an abandoned church. I ran to it. I unlocked the door and shouted, 'Hello, can anyone hear me?' I only shouted that because I heard my name being called out.

'Mia! Mia!'

'Hello, who is it?' I replied. I walked up to the altar, I felt a frosty hand on my shoulder. *What was it?* I wondered. I turned and I saw him. It couldn't be. No! It couldn't be but it was. It was my father...

'Hello Mia,' my father sobbed.

'Hello Father.' We looked at each other unobtrusively.

SOPHIE DUGGAN-CRAWFORD (11)

Dene Community School, Peterlee

THE REAPER

Immaturity, a group of teens drinking in the forest. The fog fell, they were bewildered by what was happening, then a shadow appeared out of the mist, a floating cloak, all but skeleton underneath, wielding a massive scythe with a firm grip with its cold, bony hands. Still in shock, the teens stood still, immobile but one was on the floor, passed out. She started to mysteriously rise, floating in mid-air, the scythe attacked, killing the innocent, taking souls for itself. It did this till one was left. 'Leave this place and never return or die!' Then it vanished...

ADAM THOMAS BELL (14)

Dene Community School, Peterlee

THE FIGURE

She peered through the keyhole to find a room with walls covered in blood and dirt. Peering closer, she noticed a single rocking chair, that sat on both legs rocking gently as a small brown bear tumbled over. She stood up straight and rubbed her eyes before peering back through again. This time the room turned a deep red. The lights in the room shattered; as the light slowly faded a loud thunderous scream quaked the house. She started running, she turned to face the room as a white figure with red eyes smiled at her with a sickening grin...

ELISHA HARBERTSON (14)

Dene Community School, Peterlee

THE LOST TREASURE!

On a cold, blustery night, Nathan was having a good look around the old western town but then he was startled by a roaring storm heading towards the old western town. This forced Nathan to go inside one of the buildings. As he entered the saloon there was a devastating loud noise coming from a room upstairs. He went up the stairs carefully because there were missing floorboards. He entered the room cautiously and nearly passed out due to the bad stench. There was a chest with an old artefact in it, he went to touch it and, disappeared!

TOM BROWN (13)

Dene Community School, Peterlee

SHADOW

As I awakened from my deep sleep, I glared at this horrifying shadow coming from the side of the room. I clenched hold of the quilt. With fear I jumped out of bed but before I reached the door the shadow grabbed me and clawed at my warm cheeks. I tried to shout out, it was no good, this shadow pulled me to the ground. I scuttled across the floor, my parents shouted, 'What happened, Ben?' The flashbacks made me shiver. I told my parents but they didn't believe me. They soon will though...

TODD LAWSON (13)
Dene Community School, Peterlee

HELLFIRE

I had landed. A rotting pile of corpses smeared in blood. Hoarded by the sick, twisted personification of this very place. I knew what to expect, yet I looked up and my body expelled what was left of its contents out of me. There, laughing at my weakness, hung the ceiling. Consisting of muscle. A huge compact ceiling of mutilated muscle and body, dripping blood from slithering holes. A faded red face grinned at me, large black canines showing. Its sickly thin figure tensed, ready to jump. And it did. I screamed, and it laughed - its mouth full of blood.

KEINAN ANDREW WRIGHT (14)
Dene Community School, Peterlee

THE HOUSE AT THE END OF THE STREET

In a house there was music playing. So, I slowly tiptoed into the house, the floorboards were speaking to me, screaming, 'Leave now!' I ignored it and kept walking in the front room. I saw a chair, it was rocking back and forth. I screamed, I started running then I ran upstairs. I ran into a bedroom. The sheets started moving. As I was stood against the wall I jumped then ran downstairs. The floor swallowed me, I got trapped, there was no way to get out so I screamed. No one heard. I was left screaming for help.

BETHANY ROSE PAWLEY (13)
Dene Community School, Peterlee

TRAPPED!

It was a dare, a very bad dare. Everyone left when the mist set in. They said they could see people in the distance. I thought it was only tombstones but some said it was the dead rising from their graves. *Swish.* The candles went out. The cold gripped my shoulders and I spun. Attempting to run away was not an option, it was this blocking my way out. The pitch-black, shadowy figure made its way towards me. Tombstones on all sides blocked me in. The figure slowly came towards me. Darkness. I was trapped inside the ghost.

KIERAN NEWTON (14)
Dene Community School, Peterlee

The Forest

It was dark, almost midnight. I was waiting for a cab in the middle of nowhere, all I could see was a road sectioning off my side and a lake on the other, leading to who knows where. My cab was supposed to be here an hour ago and I'm starting to get a feeling, a strange feeling... almost like I'm being watched... I ran to the left, not knowing where I'm going, but at least it's away from here. I ran into the woods only to find I'm right back where I started... I turned to find my brother...

Owen Rudkin (12)

Dene Community School, Peterlee

Isolated

I never knew how easy death would be until that day. In the misty forest, I was walking home, when I started hearing noises following me. When I rotated my head around I found where the noises were coming from. It was a shadowy, melancholy cottage. Isolated. Hidden behind the towering trees. Sauntering towards, I got closer and the noise stopped... Once I was inside, it turned silent, then I heard a whisper hurrying past my ear. I saw a black, shadowy figure. The next thing I remember, I awoke in a black insolated 'room', not remembering anything else.

Bobbi Chidley (13)

Dene Community School, Peterlee

The Man On West Street

I went missing about a year ago. He did it, the man on West Street. He killed my mum, dad, brother and me... One year before I was crying in the abandoned church when there appeared to be a homeless man stroking me, saying, 'It's OK, I know where your mother is.' He took me to the bell.

My mother was there with my dad and my brother. I tapped my mother's shoulder, she fell, her face was gone. Her eyes were gone. Blood covered the floor... That's all I remember. I'm dead... with my family...

Faith Jo Inglis (12)

Dene Community School, Peterlee

Hotel

I step through the crooked door and surprise surprise, it looks like the setting of an unfinished horror film. I turn to grab my bags, I'm startled by a black figure standing afar. Within that couple of seconds, the figure has disappeared and a scream is heard. The same black figure is racing around the haunted hotel, screams following. I spy a knife in the silhouette's hand. Edging nearer and nearer, closer and closer. I run, as fast as my little legs will carry me. But, they're faster... I can't seem to open my eyes, I'm surrounded by darkness... 'Hello?'

Megan Ditchburn (14)

Dene Community School, Peterlee

INTRUDERS

Hiding in the cupboard, it was 12:00 and I kept hearing noises. Then the silence fell, it was so quiet, I stepped out of the dusty cupboard, taking a deep breath. As I stepped out I scoped around the room, hoping there was nothing there; only rubbish and pillows were on the floor like it was before. Once I gained the courage to step further into the room, I placed my flashlight on the dusty table. Once I reached the window I noticed through the curtains. There was a man, he was staring at me with a sinister look...

SAVANNAH GEORGIA SCORER (12)

Dene Community School, Peterlee

THE VENOM OF VENICE

I stumbled across the deserted platforms of Venice. The violins played in a mocking way. Houses were sunk underwater amongst steps that led down into non-remaining towns. I was wandering around in the isolated city, searching for sources of life, but I remained unsuccessful. That's when I saw it. A human under the water, with a petrifying face staring at me, with open eyes, despite being underwater. It looked ancient. In its hand was a knife. Whether this had been a fight to keep the city alive, I didn't know. But it was staring right at me...

EDEN HADDEN (13)

Dene Community School, Peterlee

THE WHISPERS FROM MY WIFE

I saw her lying there. I froze in fear! Then I heard the whispers starting again. They were getting louder and louder. I decided to follow the eerie hallways. However, before I went I placed a kiss on her forehead. Then I ran! I could vaguely remember my way around the abandoned house from when they dragged me in; I put up a fight but I was too weak. Thoughts boomed through my mind! Suddenly, everything went blank. I couldn't remember where I was or who I was. There she was, she did this to me, my own wife!

NIEVE MORDICA (11)

Dene Community School, Peterlee

THE DARE

Thick mist settled around my feet as I entered the cemetery. Gravestones were scattered over the muddy, decaying landscape. Stone pillars entered my vision, marking my destination. Stepping into the entryway, I scanned the room. Unfurling my sleeping bag, I berated myself for accepting this dare. In the distance a clock signalling midnight, I should sleep. Opening my eyes, I glanced outside and saw twilight. I started leaving, but a whisper sounded, halting me. The whisper came again, tempting me away from the archway, towards an unusual door. Gripping the doorknob, I stepped into the passage. Everything went black...

BENJAMIN ROBINSON (14)

Dene Community School, Peterlee

The Abandoned Church

Hiding behind the corner, I saw a creature. Suddenly, I ran. The feeling was like no other, I was scared! All of a sudden I found myself surrounded by an old graveyard. Reading all the gravestones, all of a sudden I saw a big ditch. I looked down, I screamed. Down the ditch were three dead bodies. Running speedily, I came across a door. I opened the door and shouted, 'Hello? Who's there?' No one answered. I said it again and again. Then, all of a sudden, I heard a voice screaming, 'Help me!' I said, 'Who are you missing?'

Georgia Cuthbert (12)

Dene Community School, Peterlee

Laboratory Lurking

The late Dr Cameron Scott was killed in a bloody freak accident in his lab in the early 1800s. Today I was visiting that laboratory. I stepped into the lab, amazed by what I saw. It was an almost sinister feeling standing there. I slowly walked around the room, admiring items of the past. Suddenly, *bang,* the large metal doors slammed shut, trapping me, helpless. I searched around the room, looking for a way out; nothing. Then, something caught my eye - an air vent just above the professor's desk. I wiggled through to safety, or so I thought...

Caitlin Aimee Hanner (14)

Dene Community School, Peterlee

Always Getting Closer

Sliding along the muddy path, I shout for my friend, Zack, but after a while I come to a stop. I see an abandoned playground, but instead of seeing no life in this once-dormant area, I see a very pale child coldly staring at me with cold, dead, hollow, blue eyes. I slowly walk towards the 'child', still thinking about where Zack is, but when I get close to it, this child, well what I think is a child, it slowly and still yet so horrifically transforms. I start to fear for my life so I run...

Regan Whittingham (12)

Dene Community School, Peterlee

Dares

It had just turned midnight. We were stood on a field playing dares when we spotted a church which looked haunted. Nathan glared at me, 'I dare you to go in.' Showing no fear, I strolled to the door and carefully stepped in. My heart was racing.
'What brings you here?' asked the voices of thin air.
'I got dared,' I mumbled.
The lights flashed on and off. I tried to turn back but my body seemed to be glued to the dirty floor. Looking down, I was lifting off the ground. 'Say your goodbyes!'
I got dragged in. Goodbye.

Rhiannon Pye (14)

Dene Community School, Peterlee

THE WOMAN IN MY WINDOW

There is a terrible, abandoned house in the distance. I can see it from my bedroom window. I see people enter but I have never seen someone leave. Some people say it's just the house that is haunted but I think it is the whole town. A number of different deaths have happened while I have lived here but they all have two things in common. One: they have all seen the woman in the window of the haunted house. Two: they all were poisoned. I would love to finish the story but there is a woman in my window...

SARAH QUINN (12)
Dene Community School, Peterlee

TENT TRAUMA

Midnight! The moon illuminated the tent. Keeley was passed the torch. After thinking for a moment, she lifted it under her face. 'It was all quiet in the graveyard as I entered but each step made me feel more unwanted. I should've run then. Should've run when I could because now, after running for my life, I stood, unable to move, just outside the tent... And they had followed, ghosts!' She paused, Kirsty let out a loud, terrified scream and ran. It was only a story, and Lucy and Keeley couldn't stop laughing.

LUCY HARRIS (13)
Dene Community School, Peterlee

ONE DAY, ONE HOUSE

My heart was rushing, I could hear deadly noises around me. It was frightening. I gasped loudly with fear as I had nowhere to go and no place to call home. I crept closer to the wooden door. I said to myself, 'What if someone is behind there?' I could hear a record player upstairs skipping a beat every time I started to walk. I touched the rusty old door handle, shaking as I didn't know what to do, thinking what sad things could happen. As I touched the rusty door handle I stopped, then pushed it open...

DEMI TAYLOR (12)

Dene Community School, Peterlee

NUCLEAR FIRE

Underneath a thick wall of rusty debris radiated a creak of dormant machinery moving for the first time. A cog-shaped door opened, revealing a figure. The sound of a Geiger counter beeping came from a device upon the man's wrist. Emerging from the vault, he stepped into the eradicated wasteland. A green fog hung to the surface. Wind filled the surroundings with noise. Confinement clung to his chest as he stared upon the barren space. A dark shadow lurked in the fog. A scaled tail broke from the fog before being engulfed then, a deep growl came...

LUKE WILLIAMS (14)

Dene Community School, Peterlee

White House Horror

Four boys were in the woods, when they came to some steps that went on forever. However, when they got so far down they saw a mysterious white house. They made their way towards the abandoned house. When they reached it, Ashlee opened the door and it made a loud creak which echoed throughout the woods. When they entered, they separated into different rooms. However, it seemed too quiet, until Jack made a loud scream. They all hurried to him. When they found him, he had fallen into an underground cellar full of dead bodies, rats, all sorts of creatures...

Nathan Thomas Clark (13)

Dene Community School, Peterlee

Shadows

'Hush now young one.' My cyan eyes widen as I jolt out of the sickening dream that replays in my head. The darkness is enticingly calm, the warmth lulls me.
'Don't make a peep,' the darkness tells me and I begin to obey. 'Just close your eyes.'
Pulling the eye patch back over my damaged eye, its usual numbness stops and starts to ache as the other shuts.
'Let's go to sleep.' A shadow brushes over my chest and leans over me. I can feel them breathe. Letting my full body go limp, a stabbing pain hits my abdomen.

Lucy Dempster (14)

Dene Community School, Peterlee

THE HAUNTED...

I stared in the mirror. I was a demon! Just to say, I am the only one who knew. Anyway, I found this room behind the wall, which was a bit unusual. I named this room 'the secret room'. My mother and father didn't know about it either. I called my mother to check out this 'secret' room. She wouldn't dare take a step inside. I pushed her in. Within minutes she was dead on the floor bleeding. Now it was just my father left...

ELLIE WALTON (11)
Dene Community School, Peterlee

THE HOSPITAL

Clang! The car had abruptly stopped. I jerked the handbrake. 'Here we are,' I mumbled to myself. I was looking down at my twisted ankle. I stumbled out of the door and hopped through the front entrance of the grey building. As I entered, I noticed an odd unearthly smell. I tried to find assistance but no one came: except one pale young girl in a cream nightgown, sneaking toward me, mumbling. Suddenly, she darted at me, grabbing me. Everything got dark, darker, black. What on Earth? Was this Hell? No, this was the hospital, the old, neglected hospital...

DANIEL ORR (13)
Dene Community School, Peterlee

I'm Coming For You!

One spooky morning I, Issabella, woke up from a nightmare very early in the morning. I wasn't feeling myself, I went downstairs to make some breakfast but instead I got a knife and stabbed my nanna with evil laughter, 'Mwhahaha!' After that I walked out the door, over the road, and walked into the house that said: *No Entry.* I stabbed as many people as possible. Then I decided to communicate with ghosts. 'Help me be normal!'
'Go, drink blood, 3-4 sips!'
I killed an animal and drank some. After five minutes I was back to normal!

Amber Louise Travis (11)
Dene Community School, Peterlee

The Mystery Of Joel

I woke up and found myself in a dark graveyard, surrounded by old gravestones peeping up from the long overgrown grass. All of a sudden, I saw something coming out of the ground, it was a head. Wow! It was decaying, with rotten flesh and blood streaming all around. I was in shock, what could I do? It mumbled a few words, nothing that made sense to me. I tried to understand and moved closer to hear the words. Suddenly, the ground sucked up the head and it was gone. I looked at the gravestone, it was Joel...

Adam Grover (13)
Dene Community School, Peterlee

THE GATEKEEPER'S FROZEN FOREST

Joe is running and running in the legendary Frozen Forest, he's running from the Frozen Gatekeeper. Joe sprints and sprints until he finds a big round tree. He runs over to it and falls. The Frozen Gatekeeper creeps up slowly to Joe, the Gatekeeper sniffs down Joe and traps him in plants smothered in black goo. 'Where's my summoning key?' said the Gatekeeper.

Joe is then knocked out but wakes up. 'Run!' says the Gatekeeper. The Gatekeeper's icicles drop on top of Joe. Joe proceeds to run into a sword which goes through him to the Frozen Gatekeeper's heart.

AARON TUNSTALL (13)
Dene Community School, Peterlee

THE INFIRMARY

Sara clambered through the window. She'd left her keys inside the infirmary and she needed them. Quickly grabbing her keys, she left out the main exit. Her eyes caught sight of the guard's room. It was open. She entered with her heart pounding like a bolt of lightning. The wind howled as she moved the chair. There lay the guard on his back, a mouth full of blood. She panicked and ran but the door was locked. She screamed. Her patient, Jon Abruzzi, pulled out a knife. She ran but he grabbed her arm and slit her throat.

BRANDON GILLIES (13)
Dene Community School, Peterlee

Werewolf Nightmare

On a cold murky night, Olivia walked through the village's haunted graveyard on a full moon. She went in the church. There was no one there. Looking at the stained-glass windows with the moonlight gleaming in, something was there. A dark shadow was standing in front of her. She started to cowardly walk back but noticed her hands covered in dark fur. She dashed over to the mirror and realised she was the dark shadow. An almighty scream slammed the doors open. The graveyard was haunted by a werewolf. She never went again...

Molly Armstrong (13)

Dene Community School, Peterlee

A Body Of My Own

I entered the church sheepishly as it was dark. I went and found my usual seat. I heard a blood-curdling scream coming from the altar. I began to feel as if I was being watched. I paused and began to walk cautiously towards the altar. I could hear a dripping noise. I turned and there lay a bloody body. As I knelt down beside the body, I heard footsteps. It was the Devil. He shrieked, 'Don't move!' I obeyed. Turning around to face him, I felt his body enter my own. 'Finally, a body of my own!'

Nicole Rose Clarke (13)

Dene Community School, Peterlee

THE INSANE CLOWN

A curious girl crept in a mysterious building. *Slam!* The doors went. It was deserted. There was scraping of fingernails across the walls. Fresh blood dripped slowly down the walls onto the floor. She padded into a room of deadly weapons. And there, in the corner of the room of darkness, stood the crazy clown who had a smile curled from ear to ear with beady eyes. It was completely insane. It chased after her with a baseball bat with huge piercing studs that could impale you with one swing! She stopped and realised she was in an abandoned asylum!

SUSIE ASHANTI NICHOLSON (13)

Dene Community School, Peterlee

THE TAKEN KING

The Dreadnought touched down. 'This is one creepy place,' whispered Theo.

Walking down the hall, they had their guns ready. 'Grrrr,' Nathan panicked and Theo shuddered at the thought of what the noise was.

Suddenly, something dropped from the ceiling. 'W... what was that?' stuttered Bradley. Oryx, a creature from the Planet Saturn, stomped threateningly towards them. Green gunk oozed between his teeth.

'Run!' Nathan screeched.

They ran towards the Dreadnought. Firing back towards the creature Bradley managed to hit it. The rotten gunge sprayed into the air and covered them all as the door closed behind them.

NATHAN TONRA (12)

Dene Community School, Peterlee

TRAPPED

I woke up, I had been asleep for 3½ days. 3½ days into my school holidays. Tables and chairs were stacked against the wall, they looked like they were glued against the wall. Creeping out of the room, I ran towards the exit. As I opened it, it cemented shut. Trapped - like a prisoner. *Thud!* My heart was racing like the vibration of my phone. It shocked me. As I opened the text, there was a photo of me standing. I was not alone. Turning around, something covered my eyes. All I could hear was my own eerie scream.

MILLIE ICETON (12)

Dene Community School, Peterlee

THE DEVIL'S ASYLUM

I walked down the street. The moonlight shone on me like a dark spirit. It stared at me. As I approached the asylum, the whispers of death came from the wind. The streetlight burned in black flames. The trees crawled away in fear of the asylum. I entered the Devil's house, not knowing the demons inside. Wheelchairs and beds were left for dead. I walked down the hallway and the walls bled in guilt. I opened the doors. There was my family hanging from the Devil's ceiling. I dropped to my knees as he whispered, 'I want you!'

DOMINIC PEARN (11)

Dene Community School, Peterlee

YOU CANNOT DROWN YOUR DEMONS, THEY KNOW HOW TO SWIM

'Go to sleep,' I hear, but I brush it off, thinking that it is my imagination. Freezing hands brush against the skin of my arms. I flinch at their touch.

'Who? Who is there?' I open my eyes, expecting to be in my room but all I see is white padding.

'Don't you know who I am?' they ask. I gulp. 'I'm your inner demon. You've tried to drown me before, but I know how to swim.' They devilishly smirk and the lights go out. 'Go to sleep, Bethany, you'll never wake up again.'

And at that everything slowly disappears.

BETHENY HARDY (13)
Dene Community School, Peterlee

THE CHAIR

So it all started when me and my friend were walking down a hill and found a muddy path. We decided to walk along it. First mistake. We walked along this path in complete fog as we fought our way along the mud. In the distance we could see a huge house, as we came towards it the fog cleared instantly; the house was abandoned. I heard a click and I just remembered falling for what seemed like forever. As I hit the ground my eyes shut instantly. From then I cannot remember but I know I will never return.

ABBIE TURNBULL (12)
Dene Community School, Peterlee

CARNIVAL NIGHTMARE

One morning, Amelia and her friends got ready to go to the carnival. They meet at the gate for the first ride; the haunted house. As they were in their cart; they could hear voices. Their cart moved further around the house. *Boom!* There was a massive bang, the lights went off and the shutters slammed shut. Not knowing what to do, the ghosts appeared. Ghosts shouted, 'We died in here; you will too!'
People tried to get in but failed. Amelia ran and her friends followed. They tried to get out. 30 minutes later they escaped!

EMMA BIRKWOOD (13)
Dene Community School, Peterlee

THE ABANDONED FOREST

Sprinting without thinking, I ended up in one of the worst places I could have imagined, the forest! I slowly walked, my heart was beating quicker and quicker. There was an awful smell and mist surrounding me. The trees were stalking me, laughing at me! Then I saw it! The ruins of a cabin, rotted and full of fire marks. I stepped inside. Cautious and panting, I saw something. It changed me forever. Red eyes, staring directly at me, I was frozen. Stuck there... No escape.

LUKE COXON (12)
Dene Community School, Peterlee

THE CHURCH

Darkness surrounds me. I can taste the mist in the air. The church is in front of me. I go in. Candles are lighting the room. *Bang!* The door slams shut. I pull on the doorknob but it won't budge. 'Hello?' I shout. Nothing. Suddenly, the candles blow out and a maniacal laugh can be heard. Then I see a transparent figure for a few seconds, then the doors fly open and I dash out. The gravestones laugh at me and the trees shake their heads in disgust. I run home, never to return to the church.

DAVID GRANT DOVE (13)

Dene Community School, Peterlee

CREEPY HOUSE

The sun was going down, the stars were going up, I wouldn't make it out on time. Something would get me. I looked to my left and I saw a rickety old house. As I was walking over, graves were staring at me and on the floor branches were snapping. I was shivering, it was so cold. As I walked to the door I turned the doorknob. I walked up the stairs and shouted, 'Hello?' There was no answer. I shouted again, 'Hello?' I heard a noise and the door slammed shut...

DANIEL JACKSON HARRIS (12)

Dene Community School, Peterlee

DEATH BY PHOTO...

It was a warm afternoon and Lawrence Leonardson and his family waited for their plane to arrive. They were going to Florida. The plane arrived and they quickly boarded. Before they departed, Lawrence took a group selfie. But when Lawrence went to look at it, only himself and his daughter were there. The plane took off speedily. They were all enjoying the flight until suddenly there was an explosion and both of the engines caught fire. The plane crashed into the middle of the ocean. Everyone died apart from Lawrence and his daughter.

DANIEL WALTERS (12)
Dene Community School, Peterlee

HAUNTED GRAVEYARD

In the forest, there was a spooky graveyard full of mist. There were old tree branches and an old pond full of mud and dirty water. The sky was dark blue with grey clouds and scary noises. Once I saw the graveyard I noticed an old staircase. Near to the door, on the other side, there was a loud, spooky noise from underneath the floorboards. I was really scared. I didn't know what it was, so I stood still and shivered, wondering what it was.

PARIS HUNTER (11)
Dene Community School, Peterlee

TWINCEPTION

The glistening moon shone on a lad by the name of Jeff. He took strolls in the dusky woods but tonight he unexpectedly encountered a faint outline of a house. It started to illuminate to a full, plain house. Jeff phoned up his brother, Jeffrey, to get him to help explore the desolate house.

They entered, floorboards creaked with craziness, only awaiting a snap, but all of a sudden a light brightened the place. The twins decided to inch towards the light. One disappeared. A chandelier started to move. It dropped. Jeff turned around. 'Jeffrey!' said Jeff in a timid voice.

HAYDN LANCASTER (13)
Dene Community School, Peterlee

BEING FOLLOWED

As I entered the house, I could hear strange noises like the creaking of stairs and people talking behind me. When I looked around, there was nobody there. I was only thirteen and I was scared. As I walked up the crooked stairs, a door was closing by itself. I then knew it was a ghost. I tried to run but someone was stopping me. I asked who it was. 'Please stop it,' I said. It stopped. I walked down the stairs, out of the door and got back in my car. I drove away, then something strange happened...

JACK OWENS (11)
Dene Community School, Peterlee

KILLER

Harry was in his bedroom with three of his friends and they decided to go out of his boring bedroom to explore. John chose to go to an old school that his dad attended. As they dawdled up to the rusty metal gates, they could see the ancient school in front of them. 'Should we go in?' whimpered Jack as they waited at the doors.

The half-smashed door flung open uncontrollably and an eerie sound filled the atmosphere. A terrifying dark figure with bloodshot eyes came escaping out with a bloody knife. 'Dad, is that you?' whispered Harry nervously...

ABBY JONES (12)
Dene Community School, Peterlee

THE BEAST IN THE WOOD

I was thirteen when I ran away. I went into the dark forest and explored. It was midnight with a full moon. I was scared until I heard someone scream. I hid behind a tree, then saw him running. Soon I saw a beast come out of nowhere. I went to help the other man and I jumped on the beast's back. A second later it threw me off then started chasing me. I was scared. It chased me through the forest. It grabbed my leg but I got away quickly then I went home safely.

NATHAN SADLER (11)
Dene Community School, Peterlee

THE SHADOW FROM THE PAST

The atmosphere went cold. Shivers slowly ran down my spine as the wind howled like a vicious wolf. I couldn't see anything around me, just a cloud of darkness. My mind told me to walk and escape from this unknown place. But my soul told me to stay. I felt trapped inside my own thoughts and I knew I had to stay. Cautiously I began feeling around, searching for an entrance to another room. As I began moving around, I felt my eyes suddenly become heavy, almost losing my vision, struggling to keep my eyes open, a shadow appeared. Argh!

MOLLY BAIN (13)
Dene Community School, Peterlee

THE VERY HUNGRY MAN-EATING CATERPILLAR

In Peterlee there was a hungry caterpillar that was exposed to human remains. He needed more so he sought more. He was mutated into a fiercer creature! Suddenly, people were missing, their bodies eventually found in a gruesome way. The army tried to put a stop to this by nuking Peterlee. They thought it died but, unknown to them, it was in a cocoon, buried deep in the earth. Several days later, when they thought they were at peace, he hatched from his cocoon as a butterfly, destroyed Earth entirely and set out to consume other lifeforms.

JAMIE MAJOR (13)
Dene Community School, Peterlee

FLAT OUT

Toby was dead. The doctors confirmed and he was scheduled to be buried the next day. As his coffin was lowered into the ground and mud was shovelled on top, Toby opened his eyes like he'd just been asleep. He opened his mouth to scream but the weight of the mud on the cheap coffin made it collapse in on itself and him. He was too deep underground for anyone to save him and his body too full of mud to move. The last thing he saw was a large pile of mud falling on him, then a splat!

RACHEL THOMAS (13)
Dene Community School, Peterlee

UNTITLED

I wrote this to tell you what happened to me, Jonah Green. I was kidnapped at the age of 15. It all started when I was walking home and the darkness like wildfire, it created a blanket around me. I kept hearing rustling noises outside the house. I didn't dare look. There was a thud at the door. The letterbox creaked open. It started to intrigue me to go in. Little did I know what was waiting for me on the other side of the door. Suddenly, the door slammed open and I never woke again.

JASMINE HENDIN (13)
Dene Community School, Peterlee

SHADOW IN THE DARKNESS

The fog was sloping in, I was alone and the sun wanted to set. I needed to get home before dark. I saw a forest. *Going through is the quickest way home,* I thought. I ran into the mysterious forest as the fog lurked behind me. I ran through the rustic branches until I tripped on the damp floor. Suddenly, the fog caught onto me and distant crackling footsteps were around me. 'Hello?' I shouted. No reply. I shivered as I sat on a log stump. Suddenly, a figure in a black robe appeared. He walked towards me... 'Hello?'

JOSH BROWN (14)
Dene Community School, Peterlee

TRAP!

The wind was howling through the trees. The window I had climbed in had gone. I couldn't find it. Then I walked around, all I could see were dark, empty rooms. As I was in the biggest room, the door slammed shut and I could hear strange noises on the other side. I slammed against the door but it was no use, it wouldn't open up. There were no window holes or air vents! I was trapped. I searched for something to break the door but there was nothing...
Next thing I knew I was waking up near a tall figure!

JOSEPH BENTLEY (13)
Dene Community School, Peterlee

Through The Doll's Eyes!

It was snowing, Ally was playing outside and skipping through the snow. Suddenly, she stumbled across something buried in the snow. It was a doll! She picked it up to investigate. Strangely, it looked like her. She took it home and put it on the shelf.
The next morning it was gone. She felt like something was watching her. She turned around; it was there. The first thing to move was the doll's eyes! It said, 'It's your turn!' She rose up, walked over to Ally and her eyes turned red. Before Ally knew it, Ally was the doll!

Robyn Dowling (12)
Dene Community School, Peterlee

The Stalker

Walking to my house all of a sudden I heard footsteps behind me. I turned a corner and the person turned too. I looked behind me and the man was just staring at me. Uneasy and scared. I turned into a nearby forest, which was the most stupid idea of my life. I heard leaves crunching and my heart racing so fast. I saw a light in the distance and I ran towards it. Thank God, it was my house. I ran inside and shut all the windows. I sprinted upstairs. When suddenly there was a loud crash...

Ben Clough (11)
Dene Community School, Peterlee

All Alone

It was a cold, dark night, two lumberjacks were working in a forest called Thunder Creek. The lumberjacks were cutting down trees and collecting wood. They'd been working in the forest for some time, however, as this was their last night on the job they decided to stay later. As the time went by they forgot about the horrors thought to be living in the forest. Suddenly, they remembered and started running back to the car, trying not to stop. The lumberjacks were found with their skin ripped off, was this done by the horrors in the forest? Nobody knows.

Josh Anthony Lawler (12)
Dene Community School, Peterlee

Meeting The Doctor

One midnight, Tia was walking along when she saw something move. She walked into the graveyard and there was a strange man. He ran so she followed him. He was wearing a suit with a bow tie but she couldn't see his face. She walked past a blue phone box but when she returned he wasn't there. She continued walking, then she heard a wolf howling. She turned the corner and saw the man again. Standing back next to the blue box, the door opened and a bright yellow light shone out. 'Who are you?' she asked nervously...

Savannah Justine Miles (12)
Dene Community School, Peterlee

THE FOG UPLIFTS

Fog was creeping in, it was crawling up my legs, trying to pin me down. I saw my own hands float up while the fog draped round them. It started to flow around my neck, I could no longer move. It felt like something was holding onto my neck. Suddenly, I started to choke. Was someone trying to strangle me? I managed to escape by collapsing.

I woke up some time later next to an abandoned church, the fog was gone and the floor was stone dry!

JESSICA PAIGE HARDY (11)

Dene Community School, Peterlee

HE WAS THERE!

One day, while I was strolling through the woods, I saw an old and abandoned house sitting lonely on the hill. I went to investigate. The windows were black and misty but I could clearly see someone in a window. I entered the house where I then heard someone shouting from upstairs. I explored and found a man sitting in a small rocking chair. He wasn't completely there and was somewhat faded. He looked at me coldly and hopelessly. He whispered, 'Tell everyone that I was here,' and then, with that, he disappeared altogether, never to be seen ever again.

EMMA HODGSON (13)

Dene Community School, Peterlee

TRAPPED FOREVER

One foggy and misty day I was walking along my street, Sinister Street, when I noticed something strange, it was huge and very old, so I went to investigate. I walked up the steps then to the door. I went into the door and, as I started to walk up the stairs, they started to creak. Suddenly, the handrail fell off then it looked like it was getting pulled. I suddenly felt the worst was going to happen... *Bang!* The door slammed shut and I knew I was trapped forever as I heard voices saying, 'Jerry, Jerry, we will kill you...'

LIAM REMMER (12)
Dene Community School, Peterlee

THE HAUNTING

When I was walking along the path I spotted something out the corner of my eye. I crept over to see what it was, there was a tall building standing there. There were bones of dead people! As I got hold of the door handle it creaked open. I stood on the creaky floorboard, I was looking for a light. It took ages but I found it in the corner of the room. I kept walking through the different rooms. It got darker. Suddenly, I saw a white ghost floating near the ceiling...

DYLAN MATHER (14)
Dene Community School, Peterlee

IT'S REAL

She was here. I could feel her cold, ice breath. Her hands reaching out for me. I turned round, at the end of the hall she stood, her face half torn off. She grinned. I was too frightened to move. Her head was tilted, staying like that as she grinned. Slowly, she started to walk step by step...
I woke up... I got out of bed and went to the bathroom. I heard giggling, I turned on the light. She was real, she was behind me. I saw her in the reflection of the mirror... She was Carmen Winstead.

SUMMER LOUISE LEIGH (11)

Dene Community School, Peterlee

AWAKEN

I awoke in a peculiar place. The putrid smell of sweat and fear circled my nostrils. I scrambled to my feet only to be met by a spine-chilling stare. I'm not sure what was said. But what I do remember is dropping in and out of consciousness. I again awoke in what looked like a chamber. The murky walls crowded with knives, hammers, batons and all sorts of torture items. A dim fire illuminated the surroundings. The distorted figure approached me. He whispered into my ear a strange chant. Then, the greatest thing happened... I finally woke up.

CASIE-MARIE PORTER (13)

Dene Community School, Peterlee

A Night To Remember!

Fog was creeping in. I knew I wouldn't make it back before midnight. But then, out of the corner of my eye, I saw an old church. I sat on the porch steps and called Abbie. No reply. I noticed that I didn't have any reception so I tried to find a signal. I headed back towards the church doors and then appeared a doll. The doll was a little girl and she could talk. I immediately screamed, it was terrifying. Then I noticed the doll had gone. I went looking but she was nowhere to be seen.

Ellie Campbell (12)
Dene Community School, Peterlee

The Possessed

As I approached, their bloodthirsty eyes grew wider and fangs began to show. I slowly crept round their unblinking stare, not realising the ambush I was about to approach. As I neared the wall a trickle of blood ran down my leg. I then realised that the dolls were possessed. I started to run but lost feeling in my leg, sending me tumbling to the floor. I was soon overpowered by dolls with one mission: to kill me. I reached for the door to my sister's room. It was too late. She was already gone.

Leah Newhouse (12)
Dene Community School, Peterlee

THE MYSTERY CLOWN

It was a cold night and the fog rolled in through the forest. I hesitantly wandered on and came across a wooden shack. Smoke billowed from the chimney but no one lived there. Steeping into the shack, I felt the heat from the fire encase me. A clown sat looking up from the armchair. It laughed. 'Free hugs?' I ran like the wind but he was faster. He grabbed me tightly. I resisted but he was strong. 'I'm hungry!' he cackled. He tied me to a spit above the fire. I felt the heat encase me again as darkness took over.

DANIEL MARTIN (12)
Dene Community School, Peterlee

ANOTHER DAY, ANOTHER DIMENSION

Kyle slept soundly in his bed. Hands started to climb out from under it and reached up greedily for their next victim. Who knew there was a virtual transporter under the bed? Kyle woke to find himself in another dimension. Bloodthirsty demons with fangs, eyes as black as night and claws as sharp as daggers chased him. He managed to scramble away unharmed. *What is this place?* he wondered. Spotting his blanket on the floor, he shuffled under it. Kyle peered out only to recognise the comfort of his bedroom.
'Next time, we'll keep you,' a voice whispered.

KATY LONG (13)
Dene Community School, Peterlee

THE DEMONIC DOG

Harry, Daniel and Aidan were walking through the dense forest. The sky was dark and looked like it was going to rain. Suddenly, a church seemed to appear out of thin air - they ventured in. A big dog was lying dead in the middle of the floor. It was only humane to bury the poor dog. Once the burial was over it started to rain. They went inside. The children sought refuge inside the church until the storm had passed. Out of nowhere, a red light lit up the church, evil barking followed. The children were never seen again.

HARRY MASTERS (13)
Dene Community School, Peterlee

THE AWAKENING

I'm going to tell you my horrifying experience. I was walking past a part of land which was sectioned off from the village, my curiosity got the best of me and I decided to hop the fence. As I kept walking, I stumbled across two paths - a dark, mysterious path (which intrigued me) or a bright path leading back to the village. I turned right towards the darkest path. I was so scared, I couldn't see a thing until I felt something strike the back of my head and fell to the ground.
I awoke at a different location...

SOPHIE STRADLING (13)
Dene Community School, Peterlee

Dr Eading

Sarah was a lonely girl who had no friends or family. She was listening to 'Thunderstruck'. While out for a stroll lightning struck her. She woke to find herself tied to a bed with a doctor nearby, whose name tag read: 'Dr Eading'. He said nothing but pointed at a calendar. She realised she'd been in a coma for six months. She looked and saw chopped off limbs and blood everywhere then a chill crept down her spine. Quickly, he grabbed a knife and stroked her before dicing her into pieces.

Daniel Fletcher (13)
Dene Community School, Peterlee

Demon

Silence all around me. I looked around as a deep darkness surrounded me. It felt claustrophobic and, suddenly, I heard a sound from behind me. I turned around as fast as I could. Nothing was there but blackness, I heard a noise up the stairs. As I walked up the stairs the floorboards were falling through. I could hear someone up the stairs. Thoughts of who or what it could be were running through my head. As I walked through the door of the room, something was in the corner, he was very pale with bloodshot eyes...

Jack Naisbett (14)
Dene Community School, Peterlee

THE ABANDONED HOUSE

Bob was running to the closest shelter he could find. He reached an abandoned house and stayed there until the storm passed. When it was over he tried to open the door but... it wouldn't open. Then he heard a piano playing. Bob went to investigate and he froze. No one was playing it, he screamed and ran upstairs. He heard another noise but it sounded like a chainsaw. He went over and there was a man, he turned around and he kicked Bob, took his mask off and it was Bob. Bob was then killed and all evidence disappeared.

ETHAN HOWLEY (13)
Dene Community School, Peterlee

THE ABANDONED COTTAGE

As I approached the old, isolated cottage, there were loads of rats which made me jump. Although there were rats, a car had pulled up beside the cottage, it was my time to hide. I ran into the kitchen and grabbed a knife, then hid in the cupboard. I heard the door open at the back of the cottage and there were two voices and a dog barking. They went into the sitting room, so I had time to run out of the back door. I ran out of the back door, the dog was there barking...

JACK WALTON (14)
Dene Community School, Peterlee

RUBY DEATH

Mont was crouched at a lonely war site. Bombs were going off, in the air loud cries. Then... silence. Mont was confused. 'Why the silence?' Suddenly, the air filled with mist and Mont knew exactly what it was. The ruby death had come. She was a girl that had had a bomb planted in her. She died before she got to the other side. Half her face was still left on the field, but her other half and an arm were floating. She would come and drown soldiers in the mist. Mont's head blew up as if in outer space.

RUBEN ALEXANDER

Dunhurst, Bedales Preparatory School, Petersfield

IT'S COMING

Running through the seemingly endless corridors, my heart pounding. How did I get here? Never would I have imaged a few hours ago that I'd be in an abandoned mental hospital, running from... Stopping, I rested in one of the rooms. With a shock the steel door closed behind me and darkness filled the room. Panicking, I went to the door and shoved with all my might. Life or death, literally. It wouldn't budge. Tears filling my eyes, I looked around in vain for an exit when... Breathing, down my neck. This was it, the end. It had found me...

ELLA SOPHIE MCINDOE (12)

Fernhill School, Glasgow

IT'S ALL MY FAULT

I cry. I have no idea how to stop the tears from flowing. So much pain and hurt floods through my veins and into my very soul. It is then that I realise this is my fault. I'd brought this upon myself. Yet I can't find one thing to bring me back from the abyss I have created and now surround myself with. It is all my fault... His lifeless, unresponsive body lies mere inches from the blood-soaked knife held in my hand. My love, my soulmate, the very essence of who I am, dead... It's all my fault...

JODIE MANFIELD (14)
Ixworth Free School, Ixworth

THE ASYLUM

The screaming. It wouldn't stop; they said I was mad and locked me up with the insane. The damp, stone walls rang with the sound of fear and the long blank hallways were empty. Everything was silent until the night drew in. The screaming would start each and every night but tonight was different. A figure was curled up in the corner, a woman looked up, her cold bony face looked scared, scarred with tears. She screamed and would not stop, I started to scream, the walls closed in and silence fell. The asylum was still once again.

KITTY ROISIN LANGELAND (13)
Ixworth Free School, Ixworth

OUR ONLY CHOICE

It's the year 2850. A time of fear and no control over who you are. The government control everything; and we have been given the option to know our fate. I've just turned 18 and it's my turn to decide. Nothing could have prepared me for the choice I needed to make today. The book of my life - right in the palms of my hands. Should I read it? I could read it? I was told I wouldn't be able to change my fate. But surely it's possible. Knowing the inevitable. It's a scary thing... But I like scary.

BRENDA LOUISE BARROW (14)
Ixworth Free School, Ixworth

THE ROOM

A sharp pain hit my skull, paralysing my body, leaving me lying still on the stony floor. Slowly I managed to open my eyes, but only to find myself in a strange place. The room was black, with a pulsing red glow breaking through cracks in the walls. I saw something, a creature, and tried to ask where I was, but the words wouldn't come out. I realised there were more of them, surrounding me. And then I heard it, the chanting, saying one thing over and over again, each word burning my ears. 'We know what you did.'

LILLY CURRIE (13)
Ixworth Free School, Ixworth

THE GHOST

As I stood still, bats swooped over me, fog surrounded me, the graves towered over me. The graves of my family, they are not here now, but here I am, I raise my white wispy arms, praying for this torture to end. As I watch, another white figure looms over me. The expressionless face glares at me, as if all of this is my fault, both of us dead, both alive. Suddenly, he disappears, ascending to Heaven? I will never know, but I am stuck here in the graveyard, with the bats and fog, stuck as a ghost for eternity.

THOMAS HOLLAND (13)

Ixworth Free School, Ixworth

PSYCHO

Everyone thinks I'm crazy. They say I'm insane. A psycho. They don't know the satisfaction of killing someone, watching their body go limp, watching the life seep out of their eyes. Feeling the heat of blood dance across your skin, it's mesmerising. The beauty of it all; having the power to erase a person from existence in so many different ways. Power is addictive and you get hooked after your first taste. All their secrets die when you stop their heart, everything they know is no more. It's all beautifully twisted.

ELLEN DOYLE (14)

Ixworth Free School, Ixworth

THE DOOR

Along the corridor. The floorboards creaking. The eerie sound of silence, of fear, then a creak. I can neither see my fate, nor do I wish to. Nearer and nearer. The door. Anticipation, so many questions; thoughts circle around in my head. Could this be it? Do I stand here at Death's door, awaiting eternal darkness? Bemused and bewildered, I see no reason not to grasp the handle, to turn it, to open it. What could there possibly be to lose? My pride remains unchanged but my fear is growing. Slowly I push it open. Nothing. Then I'm falling. Black.

MADDIE COMBES (13)
Ixworth Free School, Ixworth

DARKNESS

Darkness stood, trying to hide from the light . A shadow, constantly chased by the sun, having to hide behind other objects. It ponders its life, thinking why so many dislike it. Why people tell stories about the dark being evil, when in fact the light is the killer. After all, darkness envelops people while they sleep. When they close their eyes, they grow to the comfort of darkness. But once again, darkness is chased, until the light ends it. It breathes, heavily, due to death drawing near. It draws its lonely, final breath.Then the whole world explodes into light.

ISAAC DALGLISH (13)
Ixworth Free School, Ixworth

WHO AM I?

I follow you everywhere you go. Yes, you. I watch you, I see every action you make, so there's no point hiding away from it. I admit, I've seen you do good, but you must admit I've seen you do bad; very bad. I record everything you do - it decides your fate. I'm your biggest fear, your worst enemy, the author of your past... but you just don't realise yet. You, yes, you, are my next victim. I, my friend, I... am your memory.

DANIEL JAMES SILLETT

Ixworth Free School, Ixworth

STRANDED

There was once a lonely lighthouse keeper who lived in his lighthouse on a small rock just off from the headland. He had lived happily for many decades until a raging storm came and waves thrust themselves against the lighthouse. He woke up to find his boat swept away and himself stranded. Days he waited until he found his water all gone and resorted to seawater. This had a disastrous effect on him. He went mad. He began seeing the men who had lost their lives, there on the lighthouse. Neither him nor his body were ever seen again.

BENJAMIN BILBROUGH (13)
King Edward VI Community College, Totnes

NEVER AGAIN

I look upon that beast of a house. I hear a twig snap. I turn sharply only to find a rabbit hopping along the iced floor. I can't help the feeling I'm being watched. *Snap!* I turn. Finding the rabbit hanged. Dead. Its days done. My heart starts racing as I walk towards the exit. That walk becomes a jog. That jog a run. That run a sprint. As I pass through the trees their branches become bony fingers trying to whisk me away from the world of the living. I look back and vow to myself, *never again*.

BLAKE MORGAN (12)
King Edward VI Community College, Totnes

WEEPING GIRL

As I walk into the abandoned village, an eerie screeching pierces my senses, like the Devil, it never stops. I look around me and there is a lonely, creaky and musty house. I decide to investigate. The walls are all wet and slimy as if it isn't quite so abandoned. On the floor is a picture; a reminder that this place was once inhabited, a sad reminder. Suddenly, a plate crashes, sending shards of glass across the room. Then the screeching stops. It's replaced with crying. There, in the corner, she sits mourning!

JACOB FINCH (11)
King Edward VI Community College, Totnes

THE EVIL OF THE SOUL

The doctor walked down the rowdy streets, his steps heavy and slow, his head throbbed. Home, he needed to go home. He must forget, forget the wickedness, the sinfulness. His bloodstained hands trembled. Blood-curdling screams echoed around him. He still remembered the ghostly white face, drained of all life. He stumbled around his dark house. The shadows mocked him. Murder! Sin! He threw off his jacket, revealing his shirt smeared with blood. He would turn in the fires of Hell! Everything went hazy, he couldn't think, nothing made sense anymore. With trembling hands he picked up the knife...

THELMA FRENCH (13)
King Edward VI Community College, Totnes

THE WEREWOLF

I'm not going to get there before moonrise but I have to. I'm in danger otherwise. I start to sprint. The dark night is brightening with the eerie glow of the moon. Twisting, turning, I feel my nose lengthening. My ribs ache, I hate this. The moon's glistening above me, mocking. I smell something. Human blood. Pounce. As the moon rises I let out an eerie howl. People say I'm mad - the Mad Moth Hunter. Full moon's the best time. A curious shape's outlined against the moon. It flies through the air. Pain. A long loud unearthly wolf howl.

KAIA LLOYD-ADMIRAL (11)
King Edward VI Community College, Totnes

LIFE AFTER DEATH

The note read: 'Death is amongst fog, serpents slither just beneath, and screams become silent'. The red paint covered the cracked walls. Lucy stared at the words. The sun came through the barricaded window. A knife gleamed, unclean. She screamed! Tears rolled down her face. *Bang!* The door collapsed. Lucy was free... or so she thought! Running fast down the damp-smelling corridor, she stopped in her tracks, facing a dingy room. There lay a motionless body. Dead? The board behind read: 'Lucy Barrot, registered 1/1/02. Death caused by suicide'. Lucy was dead! Now her soul was trapped in Hell!

VERITY SOLEY (13)
King Edward VI Community College, Totnes

MY SCREAM...

Hands shaking, heart racing, stomach churning, I reached out for the door handle. I closed my eyes and took a deep breath...
There, standing in the doorway, was a figure. A big, an unusually big figure. Its dark shadow towered over me. I rubbed my eyes. *This is a dream. This is a dream* I told myself. I told myself wrong. When I opened my eyes the figure was still there. Thunder. Lightning. He didn't move, he didn't even flinch. I didn't know what to think. Thoughts raced through my mind. Crazy, unbearable thoughts.
Silence. Then a scream. My scream.

KAREN JOHNSON (11)
King Edward VI Community College, Totnes

CHILLING TO THE BONE

Mist clung to cold air. Cold stone crumbled beneath trembling fingers. I crept through twists of ivy and creepers that spiralled up the walls of the graveyard. 'Where is she?' I asked myself. Playing hide-and-seek in an old graveyard is not a good idea, everyone knows that. The sky is inky and blotched with stars. Something moved in the shrub. 'Tash?' I called. 'Natasha?' I called again. All I could hear was the emptiness around me. Then there was a noise. I was scared now. Then came the scrambling shuffle that made me jump nervously. Game over.

BETHANY ERIN FORD-HUTCHINGS (12)
King Edward VI Community College, Totnes

THE SECOND COMING

I spun quickly, checking my surroundings. I wished I was not alone, not now... Gunshots had been fired. *Bang!* Another gunshot. I ran. But where to? Home? I kept going but then suddenly stopped. I saw a hand on the floor. The street lights came up and I saw what had been shot at. I screamed. Hands detached, feet removed from the body, then I screamed louder. I saw a disconnected head. A hand crept over my shoulder and clasped my mouth. I span. I saw who it was. It was my... my... father. And he was going to kill.

TEGAN CLARK (11)
King Edward VI Community College, Totnes

LILITH'S FRIEND

I entered the hospital. The pristine white walls enclosed me as I walked into the children's ward. I read the mental health reports. I was on duty for an orphan girl named Lilith. I entered her room.
'Why am I not treated like other children?' she whispered.
'You're treated like any other girl.'
'Don't lie to me! I only trust her, she loves me like Mumma used to...' She pointed to the corner of the room behind me. I peered over my trembling shoulder and saw two staring eyes. Then, as the clock chimed for midnight, everything went black. Silence.

SUMMER MORRIS (12)
King Edward VI Community College, Totnes

UNTITLED

My alarm went off at 3:10am when I had set it for 7:15. The old wooden chair started to rock. I started to shiver as the window opened and closed. I felt my way to the kitchen in the darkness. As I went over to the switch a flash of lightning hit the old house, sending a surge of electricity throughout the building. While all this was happening the chair was rocking more and more violently. I thought about going back to bed but then I started spinning. Faster and faster, dizzier and dizzier. Then I fell into darkness...

LOCHIE POORE (11)
King Edward VI Community College, Totnes

CIRCUS MASKS

My name's John Wickab and I just went to the circus with my son and I think a clown followed me home. Basically we got to the circus. We were inside and all was going fine until the clowns came on. There was something really sinister about them, most noticeably their masks: they looked way too red. I swear one was holding something shiny behind its back. After they finished everyone clapped apart from us because we were very creeped out. There's one now! I've just seen one! Oh God, it just broke in! It's got a...

ALFIE WAISTNIDGE (12)
King Edward VI Community College, Totnes

WOLFPACK

Thunder and lightning. Stormy night. Full moon. A dark figure lurked in the darkness of the black lifeless woods. Leaves rustled in the wind. A swing squeaked in the nearby park, swinging in the crisp night air. Ahead was the red gleam of a monster's eyes. Its howl pierced the silent night. Then, howls of its pack reacted. Six pairs of eyes, six creatures fierce and charging. Nailed to the ground, all mouths attacked me, digging knife-sharp fangs into my body. Now, my limp body lies on the muddy path of the forest. No one can find me here.

ENOLA DE JONG (12)
King Edward VI Community College, Totnes

ALONE

He sat alone, not alone but alone in his thoughts. In fact he was far from alone, he was surrounded, surrounded by the thoughts that circled his mind at night, surrounded by the emotions he felt from the moment he woke, until the moment he closed his eyes at night. You see, it felt like he was drowning but everyone else around him was still breathing. On a journey, never-ending, going nowhere. But of course, all these emotions were inside his head, out of sight, out of mind. You see, this is what it feels like, to be dead...

SASHA ALLFREY-JONES (13)
King Edward VI Community College, Totnes

THE CURTAINS

She finally found it: the key for her sister's room. Before she put the key in the lock she thought that maybe she shouldn't go in, then she remembered her sister. Slowly she unlocked the door. Everything looked the same, apart from the curtains; they used to be blue but now they were deep red. Why had they been changed? She felt a chill and assumed it came from behind the curtains. *Maybe a window is open.* She pulled the curtains back. Hanging behind them was a rope and above that rope it said: 'He did it'. Someone murdered her.

IZZY MARSHALL (13)

King Edward VI Community College, Totnes

'TWAS A STORMY NIGHT

'Twas a stormy night. The fog had descended on the village. Flashes of lightning illuminated misty tendrils swirling eerily. The pub was full. Reluctant to go outside, the villagers huddled, a dozen to a table. The bar room slowly darkened. The fire died but there were no more logs. The townspeople were drinking by two gas lamps. Candlelight bobbed out the window. It was extinguished. Thudding footsteps neared. Silence. Everyone looked to the door. Silence. Nobody spoke. *Thump, thump!* was beaten on the door. A sudden flash of lightning showed a huge silhouette at the door. It roared a deafening cry.

ELLIOTT BURROWS (13)

King Edward VI Community College, Totnes

ALONE

Children's swings creaked in the cold wind. See-saws went up and down as if someone was riding them and faint noises of children laughing could be heard in the distance. Grey wilting leaves lay lifeless on the damp ground. Stormy clouds hung menacingly low. Rain started to pour down, dampening the surroundings. An abandoned bench caught my eye. I went to it and sat down. I pulled my coat over my body and stared at the darkness. I was about to get up when a clammy, sweaty hand reached over my mouth and a rough voice said not to scream.

RIO CREED (13)
King Edward VI Community College, Totnes

BLOODSTAINS

'Mum, what are you doing up?' said a small, innocent voice. I grabbed the axe and chopped and chopped until a puddle of blood appeared. I stumbled up the blood-speckled stairs to the death-like house. I opened the door to see my peaceful victim. The odour of blood stuck to my hands. The room was small enough for a double bed. I took one last look at my victim. Once more a puddle of blood appeared. Their blood was on my hands. I remember the screams of my victims.

MOLLY CAMPBELL (12)
King Edward VI Community College, Totnes

60 Feet To Hell

The shutters on the windows flapped against their cracked frame. A chipped vase holding deformed flowers sat on the window sill. A swathe of snow blocked out the sun. A flock of geese glided past. The concrete overpass loomed over the building. She threw on her jacket and felt inside the pocket. A lighter, some cigarettes and a blood-encrusted knife. She contemplated the sharp blade and then looked out at the overpass that shrouded the marsh in a bleak shadow. She stepped outside and looked up at the drop. She didn't lock the door. She would never return.

EVE ASPLAND (12)
King Edward VI Community College, Totnes

THE MOMENT WHEN IT ALL CHANGED

I was running, I couldn't stop, I couldn't look back. People were dying because of me, because I had that stupid drink at that pathetic party. My girlfriend didn't even want to go but I insisted. Because of my nagging she lost her life. It was very sudden, my eyes were closing slowly. I couldn't control my body, my hands slipped off the steering wheel. My girlfriend's screaming was blocked out by the alcohol. That's when we hit the truck. It wasn't their fault, it was mine. I won't even deal with the consequences, I just can't.

ROBIN POYNTER TAYLDER (11)
King Edward VI Community College, Totnes

THE NIGHT

'I can't run forever, it will catch up. It's here, what do I do? *No!*' That was a diary entry from two months ago. The body was never found, but that desolate house remains. Unfortunately that wasn't the last time someone went there. Her name was Sasha, she entered the house yesterday. I was there, I saw it. At first the house was still but when night came it brought evil with it. I ran into a room, the door slammed. I heard screaming! The shadows loomed over me. I survived, but not Sasha. I tried to help. Poor Sasha.

BENJO APTROOT (13)
King Edward VI Community College, Totnes

THE MAZE

He went to sleep knowing it was safe and warm. When he woke up he realised he wasn't anymore, he was cold and scared. He climbed out of bed and noticed the floor wasn't carpet, it was stone and there was no wardrobe, just stone walls. Except for straight ahead. Slowly he tiptoed backwards, but where he expected the bed to be it wasn't. He fell over and crawled backwards, he screamed as a hand touched his shoulder. He ran forwards, still screaming, screaming until, *thunk!* His head fell as his body carried by his momentum stumbled forwards in silence.

CHARLIE JONES (13)
King Edward VI Community College, Totnes

THE MURDERER

I heard the sound of glass breaking. I ran upstairs and hid in the bathroom. Sophie was hiding under the stairs. I prayed Sophie would be OK. I heard drawers being opened and rummaging downstairs. Then there was silence. Suddenly, I heard Sophie scream the most stomach-turning scream. More silence. I heard the back door unlock, open then close. I waited for what felt like an eternity. Finally, I crept downstairs into the kitchen and fell to the floor. Sophie was lying there. I felt her hand. Ice-cold. 'I'll kill whoever did this to my wife,' I swore.

MARIA MORLEY (12)

King Edward VI Community College, Totnes

DISAPPEARANCE!

The old floorboards creaked with every step Ellen took, until she stopped walking. As the door slammed shut they studied the room carefully and casually. Suddenly, a girl sang in the room but they didn't see her, they could only hear her laughing cheerfully and singing calmly. Now there was only two of them, calling for their disappeared friend. Then there was only one girl. Then zero. The only thing that could be seen were three little dolls sat on the dusty fireplace singing and laughing quietly. If you come close you can hear their little voices.

ALANA WELLS (12)

King Edward VI Community College, Totnes

DOLLY

In the rain, as the wind swept the hair out of my eyes, I noticed a china doll leant up against a stone wall. An old woman came out of the museum and glanced at the small doll. She stumbled down the steps. She picked the doll up and threw it in the bin. She then walked by, as if nothing happened. Ignoring the memory of her worried face, I went over and took it out. I then walked home. I was woken by a violent scream and the doll at the end of my bed. Then nothing but darkness.

RHIANNON POPE (13)

King Edward VI Community College, Totnes

SILENCE

The rapids I'm wading through turned my legs numb hours ago. Suddenly, the racing water turns still and silence floods the cave in an overwhelming wave. Just silence. Silence. The sheer force hits me and I'm almost knocked over. Then I realise the rising water is petrifying my body until nothing can move. The only thing I feel is the locket I found, heating my skin against the bitter water. The next thing I know, water fills my lungs, my feet lift. As my vision goes and everything turns black I can hold it no more. The locket drops.

AMÉLIE EASTON (12)

King Edward VI Community College, Totnes

CRASH

Crash! A loud sound wakes you up from your sleep, you decide to go outside to investigate. The moment you step outside you can already feel the heat of fire. You walk towards it, despite the heat and notice it's a car crash. The door on one of the cars is open from the heat. You see a burning body still holding the steering wheel. Curiosity gets the better of you. You want to check the other car. Fire bursts from inside the car. You launch back from the heat and in horror, sat in the seat, is your burning corpse.

LEWIS CORLETT (13)

King Edward VI Community College, Totnes

ONCE UPON A GRAVE

'I dare you to lie on one of the graves,' Dani shouted to Emily.
'Only if everyone does,' she replied.
'OK.'
'One, two, three.'
Now Emily stood at the foot of the grave she was to lie on. 'Mia Elleson' the gravestone read. The grass-covered grave was cold and lumpy but Emily didn't care. *Plop!*
'Argh!' Milly screamed and was gone.
'Argh!' Emily now found herself screaming, then suddenly cold hands grasped her arms.
'I am Amy, would you like to play?' a faint voice whispered in her ear.

GIORGIA CORNISH (11)

King Edward VI Community College, Totnes

NEEDLES

'Don't stop, keep running.' The grass slashed my bare feet. I ran, heart thumping, veins at the edge of bursting. My legs grew heavier with every step. My right foot collapsed. I stumbled over roots. Thorns ripped at my flesh. Instincts took over. Everything was dark but I knew what'd happened when liquid dripped down my hands. I felt a sharp point and I knew life was over. On the leaves and thorns beyond the canopy above, ignoring pain, rustling steps kept closing. Before closing my eyes I glimpsed the shadow looming over me. Nails piercing my skin.

EVELIN SWOBODA (13)
King Edward VI Community College, Totnes

LURKING SHADOW

12pm, I lay down on my creaky bed, closed my eyes and drifted off to sleep. Just then I felt a flowing breeze drift past me, I opened my eyes. With horror, I was lying next to a tree inside a graveyard with the church in the distance. The sky was cloaked with clouds and the trees were blowing in the whistle of the wind. I slowly walked up to the church and opened the big wooden door. I stepped into the dark, draughty room. Just then the candles blew out, as a cold, white hand touched my shoulder.

BROOKE TOMS (12)
King Edward VI Community College, Totnes

THE LETTER

Today's the day that will decide my life. He's coming. Everybody calls him by a different name: Darkness, Soul Reaper, Fate. He gives you a letter, you hold time in your hands, when you are thirteen the letter tells you how much time you have in the world. A boy was dead before he hit the floor. Cold, lifeless, that's what he became.

Today is my day. He's at the door. He gives me the letter. He's dressed in a brown, degraded coat with wooden toggles. He wears a black mask. He leaves and I open the letter. So soon...

BENJAMIN SUMMERS (13)
King Edward VI Community College, Totnes

THE GHOST OF ECHO HILL

Suddenly, the door slammed behind me and the screams stopped. When I tried to call Max the call didn't go through as I expected. Now I was stuck with a murderer as my only company. Suddenly, my phone rang and Max said he would be there in 20 minutes. The moment I hung up the screams started again but I was too scared to look. As thunder and lightning danced in a storm I felt a stone-cold hand on my shoulder. 'Max, are you there?' I asked. 'Max, this isn't funny. Max?' That was the last thing I said.

OLIVER HARRIS (11)
King Edward VI Community College, Totnes

THE REFLECTION

The girl was there. Her spine was full of shivers like stabbing knives. The voices in her head shrieked in pain. The room was intense. In the moonlit room clowns hung, strangled by ropes and chains tied to the door. There was no escaping. Her heart pounded as she turned to a broken mirror in the distance. She peered into it and in the far corner two golden, spiteful eyes peered back at her, unblinking. Then a hand came. A shriek. Nothing. There wasn't anything but a trail of blood left, even to this day.

JASMINE BROWN (11)
King Edward VI Community College, Totnes

THE SCREAM!

This was the first time I had been to my friend's house. I walked in the door and instantly felt a thousand eyes watching. The door slammed behind me. 'Alice!' I shouted. She wasn't there. 'Alice!' I shouted louder this time. So I went on a hunt to find Alice. As I went I could hear tiptoeing, then there was a scream. I thought it was Alice so I shouted, 'Alice!' and ran towards the scream. My heart was beating fast. My heart started beating faster and faster. I felt someone tap my shoulder. It wasn't Alice...

ABBI BAKER (12)
King Edward VI Community College, Totnes

RUN

He'd been walking when he heard the scream. He turned around to see a woman on her knees. White eyes, pulsating pupils, a veiny face. She was on the floor, like she was having a fit. Then, suddenly, she stopped, looked up and screamed. She spotted the man and smiled gleefully. He ran. He turned into an open door and locked himself in the bathroom. *Thud!* He looked for an escape. *Thud!* He felt dizzy. *Thud!* He started to throw up, knowing there was no way out. The door opened. He cried. He whimpered as she leapt towards him.

CIARAN FINN-LOOBY (13)
King Edward VI Community College, Totnes

NIGHT AT THE CEMETERY

Walking in the darkness, not wanting to open my eyes. Dared to spend the night in a cemetery, well I couldn't let my friend think I was a wimp, could I? Hearing noises that give me goosebumps, I decide this really is no fun. *Stop being silly,* I tell myself, *just open your eyes.* So I stand in the darkness and open my eyes. I felt sick with fear, shaking from head to toe. All I could see were figures, figures that were coming towards me...

JAYDEN PAXTON (12)
King Edward VI Community College, Totnes

LOST AT SEA

I awoke to the feeling of bobbing like my body was floating. I tried to move my left leg but I couldn't. It felt stiff. I then tried to move my arms, first my left then my right, they felt heavy. After lying still for a few minutes I could finally sit up. I looked around and all I could see was blue. I was alone at sea. Wandering around this mysterious vessel I discovered nobody was onboard. The last thing I remember was me walking the streets of Paris. I had no idea where I could be.

HENRY MORGAN (13)
King Edward VI Community College, Totnes

CLICK

Rain is falling as we sprint towards the house. We burst in. Blackness. I find my torch, illuminating the room. It looks like someone lives here. A sound comes from upstairs. Two of us go up. Upstairs there are two bedrooms. *Click!* A key turns in the other door. My friend's stuck. *Smash!* Then a scream. The door swings open. She's dead. *Click!* Downstairs there's another scream. Blood leaks from under the door. Then my door slams shut. *Click!* It locks. I run to the window, my only escape. It grabs me. Too late.

HARLAND CLARK (13)
King Edward VI Community College, Totnes

HE'S BEHIND YOU

The silver disk hangs alone in the star-dusted sky. The moon is glaring at me as beams of light illuminate my bedroom. The air is unusually cold. Chilling. I'm not alone. I look behind my shoulder. Nothing's there. Eerie silence fills the room like the deceased-filled graves. Morbid thoughts flash through my head hastily. The walls whisper, 'He's behind you. Behind you!'
Am I imagining this? Am I dreaming? Overwhelmed I run to the door. I pull it hard. It won't open! 'Please help me!' I scream. It's then I see his breath on my neck...
'Behind you.'

AMELIE NORAH O'LEARY-BLACK (13)

King Edward VI Community College, Totnes

YOU'RE NEVER ALONE

You run. It's coming! You reach the door. It's locked. You turn around. Off again. It's getting closer! Into the kitchen, locking the door, you hear it scratching. You try the windows. Locked. You're trapped! 'I'm coming,' you hear behind you. You turn around. There it lurks, silhouetted. You reach the door. It's jammed. You're stuck. It's closer. Something grabs your arm. It's cold. You scream, try and punch, but it pulls you, laughing. You break free, dive into the cupboards. You hide. 'Where are you?' *Bang!* 'Found you!' You scream and kick. It bites! 'Goodbye!' Death ends your suffering.

JAMIE MEDD (13)

King Edward VI Community College, Totnes

The Wolf

The mask goes on. The gloves too. A wolf stares at me. It picks up the axe, covered in blood, and spreads across the front door. It breathes heavily and runs forward. Suddenly, the door bursts open! I see nothing. I run out and stumble down the grass hill. I get in my car and drive far away. After five minutes I see something strange in the back of my car. I catch a glimpse of a wolf and then gloves. The street lamp turns off. A claw slits my throat. My scream fades away, into the dark, dark night.

Mac Toler (13)
King Edward VI Community College, Totnes

My Shadow

The shadow follows me every day. It's there in the worst of situations and it ruins the best. It looks at me with its cold, almost black eyes and shakes me to the core. My shadow is beautiful but brutal; a butterfly on a summer's day and a wolf on a crazed hunt, simultaneously. It's my only friend but it ruins me. At night, when the moon is full, it's there. Waiting in the corner, a swollen black mass slowly reaching for me, whispering in the dark, a comforting tune, cradling me close. Everyone has a shadow. Where's yours?

Camille Street (12)
King Edward VI Community College, Totnes

THE ASYLUM

I woke up in the asylum to dark, eerie hallways, the sound of
screams drawn to my ears. The stench of rotten flesh and death
lingered. Being back in that place! Walking. Breathing. Smelling.
Like I belonged there. The building was in pieces. There was a
memory I can't forget. I went onto the roof and stood at the edge.
I jumped...
I wake up all hot and flustered. I have had a hard time and I don't
want to live. So I'm going to the bridge to jump. Goodbye.

LUCY PHILLIPS (12)

King Edward VI Community College, Totnes

HORRID HENRY!

In this dark room the queer old man that goes by the name of
Henry sat in his creaky rocking chair, staring at the smashed
window, shivering. The light blue in his eyes showed that he'd
seen better days. There was a reason why he was in this room!
Pale dead bodies lay around the house inside and outside, with
the fresh, bloody wounds round their necks looking like bite
marks. No wonder Henry has these horrid, red-coloured metal
spikes in his mouth. Well, the question is, why does he do this?

JONJO HAWKSWORTH (12)

King Edward VI Community College, Totnes

IN THE DARKNESS

It is Friday the 21st. I'm in darkness. I remember being in my house on Elhme Street. The lights started to flicker. There was a new feeling in the room. A presence. Then suddenly, with a loud crash, all went dark. My eyes are still in darkness but occasionally the lights flicker on then off. Each time the lights turn on it's blinding, like the face of the sun is centimetres away from my eyes. I feel an arm glide along my back and then pull on my hair. 'Help!' I scream. I'm losing all hope in this darkness.

LILY EDMUNDS (12)
King Edward VI Community College, Totnes

PINS AND NEEDLES

That needle had consumed him, he went from a violent struggle to a twitch. The surroundings darkened and each shadow blended in. Although I was next I desired to see beyond the way I perceive this world. I was changing and the pain was unbearable. Soon my eyelids closed. It all went dark and my blood was cold and painfully slow. Although I had regained consciousness I would soon sleep again, forever. The struggle to keep my heart beating led to something much worse. I had closed my eyes again.

FINLAY SURGEON (12)
King Edward VI Community College, Totnes

THE DARK SHADOW

The stairs creak as a shiver travels slowly up my spine, making my hairs stand up on end. My cold, pale face peeps around the corner as I wonder what is going on. The tall, black walls are cold as I put my hand out to touch them. Suddenly, a blast of icy, crisp air blows through my hand; whispering winds ripple around the shadow-filled room. There's a smell of dust that has been ageing on the fireplace for years. The door creeps open. It's just a black cat that paced across the room slowly as I sigh with relief.

CARYS TRUMP (11)
King Edward VI Community College, Totnes

DETECTIVE WALLACE AND THE CHAINSAWS

One misty evening Detective Wallace was out scouring the moors for potential leads on the recent murders when something caught his attention. He saw a padlock on the floor and a shed door open, full of bloodstained chainsaws. As he examined the shed, at that moment, he heard the sound of a running chainsaw. He looked back and saw a tall and shady figure approaching him. He ran inside the shed and shut the door but chainsaws can cut through wood...

JACOB SMITH (12)
King Edward VI Community College, Totnes

KILL OR KILLED?

There was once a girl who went to a doll shop to look for a Halloween doll so she could draw it. When she got home it was 11pm so she went to bed, put it on her desk and went to sleep. She felt something moving on her bed. It was the doll! She ran into her mum and dads' room but they weren't there. She ran downstairs. She heard, 'La la la la...' The doll was on the stairs, walking to the girl, singing, 'La la la la...'
She screamed. Then silence.

ELENA ALDRED (11)
King Edward VI Community College, Totnes

IT

I was tired, too tired, but I had to keep going. My legs were burning from the endless running. I was getting nowhere; only the same vast, empty darkness. Nowhere to hide, nowhere to go. It was closing in. My body shook with both pain and fright. It was going to catch me. I felt like collapsing. I could feel its breath on my neck. I couldn't keep going. What was the point? My legs buckled and I fell. I expected it to grasp me with its bony fingers but I didn't hit the floor, I kept falling, falling, falling...

IZZY WALTON (12)
King Edward VI Community College, Totnes

THE HOUSE

I walked down the dark, gloomy corridor, when I saw a faint glow coming from one of the bedrooms. I peered through the ancient door. It made a quiet creak as I opened it. A thick mist poured out of the room. As the fog cleared I noticed that in the corner of the room there was a bed and on the bed there was an old, shrivelled hag of a lady. She turned to look at me and reached out her hand. Fire shot out. The flames licked around my face and I felt searing pain. Then nothing.

ISAHIA CHAUVE (11)

King Edward VI Community College, Totnes

ALONE

Looking around I wondered where I was. Wherever it was it smelt of rot and burning. 'Argh!' Suddenly, I heard a scream.
'Hello, anyone there?' Suddenly, a laugh came from behind, quickly turning around I saw a shadow. I repeated, 'Hello, anyone there?' No answer. Then the door in front of me swung open. 'Come this way.'
Hearing the banging of lockers, I followed. I stopped in the hall, seeing flashing images of people suffering, making me dizzy. Slowly opening my eyes I got up and walked to my right. Out of the corner of my eyes, there it was...

ALEXANDER SMITH (12)

King Edward VI Community College, Totnes

THE MANSION

It was there. He knew it. He couldn't build up the courage to turn around. He could hear the terrified screams of his friends. He finally got the courage to slowly turn around. Before he could move he felt his legs get stiffer, harder even. It felt as if the walls were closing in. As soon as he thought this he saw a body drop from the ceiling... Hanging from a chain. He ran as fast as he could. He stumbled out of the room into the garden outside. There he saw the hands of statues pointing at him.

REECE LILLEY (11)
King Edward VI Community College, Totnes

THE WALLS

The walls crack, dust rains from the broken roof and glass shatters from the whistling wind. Quiet whispers echo around the room but there is no one to be seen. This haunted classroom slowly falls apart, screeching tiles slide off, the sharp pillars that surround the room. Is there someone here? I walk towards a bent chair. It rumbles. 'What's there?' A little metallic ball rolls out. I jump. Suddenly, I hear a slight rattle. I look behind but nothing's there. I look forward. The metallic ball has disappeared, nowhere to be seen. Where has it possibly gone? *Screech!*

JOE CORBETT (11)
King Edward VI Community College, Totnes

FIRE-EYED

If the world ends I hope it ends with fire. Fire, the scorching beast, the flaming torturer. The one who kills. Slowly. Painfully. Without mercy. Yes, I hope it ends with that. I hope it ends with screams of agony and cries to God. The world deserves to burn. I will kill them with fire so I can watch them writhe in pain and shout for mercy. I smile menacingly at the thought and tilt my head back; snap open my eyes and glare. A strong bloodthirst dries my throat. This is what it means to be fire-eyed...

CATHRYN HONEY (12)

King Edward VI Community College, Totnes

THE TRIP TO THE BEACH

Slowly walking down the rough, sandy path, Jasmine said, 'Come on!'
We both started to run down the lane. 'Wait!'
'What now?' said Jasmine.
'Come out!' *She'll come out soon*, I thought, feeling a dark shadow slip down the path.
'Run, quick! Down the lane, to the sand!' I screamed.
Sliding, running quicker and quicker. I instantly felt the deep fear slide inside my soul. Run quicker, faster, you'll be fine. 'Please, just don't let it hurt me,' I begged. A shack was in the distance. My feet trembled. Fear came closer. Everything came together. The shadow came closer. 'No, please...'

EVIE BOVEY (11)

King Edward VI Community College, Totnes

THE LAST RIDE

He opened the door and got into the car. Whiskey and a handgun rode shotgun instead of his daughter. He didn't stop until he got where he was going. Nowhere. He took a final swig of his drink and stepped out of the car, loading a single bullet into the chamber. He looked up at the delicate night sky, and then fell to his knees, shaking. 'I'm coming, Adi,' he spluttered between sobs. He drew his last breath. *Click! Bam! Crash!* He always wanted her to be the last thing he would see before he died. Another gone forever. Alone.

POPPY PAYNE (13)
King Edward VI Community College, Totnes

THE GAME

Shirley and her brother James were at the doctors waiting to find out if they could get the money to fund James' cancer operation. A strange man told her she could win the money. Later on that night Shirley went to the man's house. There were others there. They played a serious game of 'would you rather?' All of the people there needed the money for different reasons. A man stood up and tried to escape but a waiter shot him and dragged his body out of the room. Everything went silent. Only two people were left, one could leave.

ELLA MILES (12)
King Edward VI Community College, Totnes

Running Like Never Before

The light was fading fast. Sweat bled from my skin causing my hair to stick, as my throat pined for air. The track became a blur as my adrenaline urged me on. There was no time to look back. I had to get away. I stopped for a moment to catch my breath. All I could hear was my pulse beating furiously in my ears. 'Well, well, well, looks like you've found us.' I stood, paralysed, and felt my once agile legs crumble beneath me. For the first time in my whole life, blackness engulfed me like a warm blanket.

Martha Davies (14)
Queen Mary's School, Thirsk

Hanging

'Keep it together!' Tentatively I stepped out of the strangling fog. 'You can do it.' Taking small steps I was seriously contemplating whether to turn back. Shadows cast by trees reached out and danced. A cold hand on my shoulder brought me back to reality. A hand! Determined, running, panting; the church emerged out from the shadows. Slowing down, gradually halting. Carefully and cautiously peering over my shoulder. Big, big mistake! Hanging from the great oak tree lay a child's doll. Smiling! With no other option, my body was running in the direction of the abandoned church. Darkness.

Angel Barton (14)
Queen Mary's School, Thirsk

THE SHADOW

The charcoal greyness glistened in the midnight moon creating a monstrous shadow on the path below. No light nor people were ever seen. My footsteps echoed amongst the seething silence of the dead below. Through the haze I saw a blob, that became a figure that became a woman. A large golden shovel stood meaningfully in her hand. Only noticeable as it was smothered in the redness of blood. A wave of terror washed over me. I began to run. Long infected hands clasped me. The blurry woman was clear in the face as she drew the shadowy shovel.

SOPHIE EMMERSON (14)
Queen Mary's School, Thirsk

THE WENDIGO

I switch on my torch and open the door. I step into a corridor. All the doors are closed but one. Ignoring my trepidation I slowly edge towards it. It leads to a cellar. My torch starts to flicker; at the bottom of the stairs the door slams behind me. The beam of my torch lands on a corpse; it's the missing girl reduced to little more than bones. My torch dies, I panic, frantically tapping the torch. I hear footsteps coming closer. My torch comes back on. A mutilated, sallow face of a demon is inches from mine.

HARRIET SMITH (13)
Queen Mary's School, Thirsk

TAKEN

'He's taken another girl,' said the officer, who was standing in front of us, staring intently into my eyes. 'It's even more important now than ever that you communicate with us,' he continued, 'tell us everything there is to know.'
My stomach dropped. The blazing fire suddenly turned ice-cold, freezing me like a statue with only memories that I never wanted to think about again surfacing in my mind, driving me insane. My eyes darted around the room flicking from the officer's stern face to my mum's fearful one and then to the warm, gentle hand that clenched mine...

INDIA TURTON (13)
Queen Mary's School, Thirsk

SHE'S HERE

My first investigation, I had been sent to seek a child who went missing three years ago. I approached a rotting barn. This is where walkers heard screaming. The stench hit me first. Then the bones, knives and blood. Suddenly, the door slammed and locked. I spun round the room, gun at the ready. Stood in the doorway was a small girl. No eyes, long hair, soaked in blood. I ran to cover, when I looked back... she was gone. The last thing I remember is a cold, wet hand, wrapping round my neck, and the sound of piercing screams.

NERISSA SHUTT (14)
Queen Mary's School, Thirsk

BLOODTHIRSTY

Blood dripped down walls and swirled among smashed glass. The bodies I had so heartlessly murdered lay strewn across the bloodstained carpet. Outside the wind howled and fog drowned everything in its path. I glanced around, saw no one, so plunged my sparkling fangs into a still fiery heart I'd ripped from some poor soul. I moved out of the restaurant with my sack full of organs, along the alleyway and into my next target shop. I wandered in, hair drenched, make-up running. Staring around I picked out my victim, grabbed my throwing knife. It flipped forward...

MEGAN MARSHALL (14)

Queen Mary's School, Thirsk

TIME FLIES

I had at least three hours to live, well at least that's what my doctor told me. You should never trust doctors, my roomy was told she had thirteen hours, she lasted three. The white hospital walls around me caved in, they had tried to make light of the room with pictures, I can't say it worked. There it is again, the soft but increasing scratching noise. The feeling of being watched. The room felt tight but that was nothing compared to now. Looking at the clock, seeing the time: shock. Think I'm writing this now? Wrong. I just died.

MEG OLIVIA FORD (13)

Queen Mary's School, Thirsk

THE HOSPITAL

I walked into the abandoned hospital. Chills went down my spine. A doctor appeared in old clothing. I was told to follow him. I was in an operating theatre. A nurse brought over a needle. She injected me. I drifted to sleep. The lights flickered, blood poured from the walls. I tried to get up but I couldn't. I was paralysed. The doctor whispered in my ear, 'This will not hurt.'
I tried to scream but no sound came out...

MATTHEW OAKLEY (13)

Sandwell Community School - Wednesbury Campus, Wednesbury

PIRATES - SOULS OF THE SEA

It was a stormy day on my ship when a Spanish galleon appeared. Within a few seconds cannon shots were fired. We all knew we didn't stand a chance yet we continued fighting. Our ship was broken, sails torn then he boarded! The captain, pale and ghost-like, walked up to me with his diamond-encrusted sword. I pulled out my flintlock pistol and shot right into his chest but he carried on! He ran at me, twisting his sword through my stomach. 'You now belong to the souls of the sea,' he whispered, as I took my last breath.

HARRY PADDOCK (14)

Sandwell Community School - Wednesbury Campus, Wednesbury

THE HOUSE

One evening three children were playing football. All of a sudden the ball went over deadman's territory. None of the boys would enter there. A family lived there ten years ago. Rumours are that one night their little boy woke up screaming. His mother checked on him. Returning to bed she realised her husband was missing. They all disappeared. No bodies were ever found. The boys jumped the fence and spotted their ball. Suddenly, they saw a shadow in the bedroom window. They went to investigate. Together they entered the house. They never returned...

NATHAN SUTTON (13)

Sandwell Community School - Wednesbury Campus, Wednesbury

FREEDOM

The steel felt hard and cold in my hands. I felt a shiver through my body. The cell door unexpectedly opened. I've been in prison over thirty years. It's all I know, the real world scares me. I look to see if anyone's around, the place is silent. Cautiously I tiptoe into the corridor. I'm shaking uncontrollably with fear. I feel a hand rest upon my shoulder. Someone or something whispers in my ear, 'Come with me and find your freedom!' Do I go or remain in the safety of the prison walls?

ASHLEIGH GLOVER (14)

Sandwell Community School - Wednesbury Campus, Wednesbury

THE CRYSTAL

As the moon shone I walked slowly into the forest. The fog surrounded me, my vision distorted. Something seized my leg from the undergrowth. I was dragged down into the Underworld. Suddenly, a gleaming light burnt my eyes. A voice exclaimed, 'You are the chosen one!'

Why me? I was born for a reason, to kill! In my clenched fist was a neon crystal. This crystal's soul purpose was to wipe out the planet. With a flash I was transported back to the forest. I was dazed! I uncurled my fist. What would I do?

TAMMEM MIAH (14)

Sandwell Community School - Wednesbury Campus, Wednesbury

MISSING

Whoosh! Wind whistled through the creaking branches, bells rang out in the dark distance. As the lightning clashed the children played in an old disused hospital. Running towards the lift, the doors slowly opened with a screeching noise. The children laughed, they happily walked inside, not realising what they were getting themselves into. Pressing random buttons they slowly rose, then the lift stopped! Gradually the doors opened. The long, dark corridor was enveloped in silence. The children stared and walked from the lift. A scream raged towards them! They looked around. One of them was missing...

MIA MORANO (12)

Sandwell Community School - Wednesbury Campus, Wednesbury

Zombie Boy

Bod suddenly woke up needing the toilet. He got up and walked down the cold, dark hall and started to go downstairs. Halfway he slipped, and *crack!* His head landed on a needle. He started to have a seizure. He turned green! He sprinted upstairs screaming. His family woke up. His mom checked his temperature but he bit her face. Then he bit his nan. His nan feasted on the dad's brain. They left through the front door and began to feast on the world...

COLHUM HELLIER-CAMPBELL (12)

Sandwell Community School - Wednesbury Campus, Wednesbury

The Haunted Palace

John was having a sleepover for Bob's birthday. They had intended playing Xbox all night, but it had broken. Boredom had struck and unsure what they could do, they decided to go for a walk. As they were walking through the forest, they saw an abandoned palace. They decided to start walking through the old palace. As they entered one of the rooms they found a gun and a torch next to a dead police officer. They picked them up slowly. All of a sudden John dropped to the ground. He had no pulse. Could he be dead?

KRISTIAN GAUNTLETT (13)

Sandwell Community School - Wednesbury Campus, Wednesbury

You Shouldn't Have Come Here!

We'd just moved house, me, Mum and Dad. The new house was tall, ancient and narrow, and whenever I went inside I shivered. One night I was left alone, I sat there in the living room, watching TV, when suddenly it turned off. I got up to look behind it. The plug was on the floor. I was very confused. I plugged it back in and sat down. A few moments later it turned off again. However, this time I didn't have to get up. It turned back on itself. Reading the words across it: 'You shouldn't have come here!'

Katie Rogerson (11)

St Edmund Arrowsmith Catholic High School, Wigan

The Mirror

She looked up, turned around and then noticed a door hidden behind a piece of silk. She ran over to it, removed the silk and opened the door. She stepped inside with her heart in her hands. It was empty, apart from an old, dirty mirror stood in the corner. She couldn't help herself but to shut the door and look into the mirror. She took a step closer to see if the floorboards were creaky, but they weren't. She walked over to the mirror and saw her reflection in it. The last thing I remembered was her voice, screaming.

Niamh Harrison

St Edmund Arrowsmith Catholic High School, Wigan

DEAD AS NIGHT

As I eased towards the edge, I spotted what looked like a scene from an exaggerated drama unfolding on the street below. I needed to help. I nervously, yet quickly, scuttled down the bell tower and sprinted to the scene. It was a mess: the murderer wasn't stopping after killing one man.

After a pause for breath he turned to me with a psychotic smile. Leaned down... The warm blood dripped onto me from the knife held close to me. I braced and looked away.

There lay the first victim: cold and helpless. Was I the next?

JESSICA PILKINGTON (13)
St Edmund Arrowsmith Catholic High School, Wigan

THE ANONYMOUS INVITATION

It was the darkest hour when I stood at the door. The anonymous invitation had brought me to an abandoned house. I knocked on the door. *There'll be no answer*, I thought, I was wrong. The door slowly creaked open. I called into the house but there was no reply. I called again but still, no reply. I grabbed my flashlight out of my pocket and took one step into the house. I took another step in and the door slammed behind me. I tried to open it but it wouldn't budge. Suddenly, a cold hand grabbed my shoulder.

ALYSSA PARKER
St Edmund Arrowsmith Catholic High School, Wigan

THE END

If only people cared. If only I meant something to someone. It's not like it would matter if I was gone. I'd be shocked if they noticed. Even my own mother, the person that gave me life, couldn't care if I was gone. She... hurts me. My father's been dead for years but even if his corpse was still walking he'd probably want me in the furthest grave away from where he stands. The bullies, all they care about is how I look, how I act but it won't make them change. Even living I'm dead to them...

SHAY GAUGHAN-ROLLS (13)
St Edmund Arrowsmith Catholic High School, Wigan

MISSING GEORGIA

Georgia and I went out. We lived by a haunted castle, some people say. I got a phone call, so I turned away. When I turned back Georgia was gone with the castle door wide open. I crept inside and started to call her. 'Georgia!' No answer so I tried again. 'Georgia.' Still no answer. Suddenly, I heard footsteps. 'Georgia,' I called. At this point I was petrified. Suddenly, I saw a shadow, it was coming nearer and nearer. All I could think was, *What is this? Is this Georgia?* I turned around. In my face was something petrifying...

KATIE MCGRATH
St Edmund Arrowsmith Catholic High School, Wigan

FACES

Everywhere... everywhere I look... there's no escape... this is where it ends...

I wake up from a crazy, insane night of pranking young, innocent and frightened kids, telling them they would die on Halloween. I can hardly breathe... A hand covers my mouth... Not much to see; the plain ceiling and a humongous man covering my mouth, watching over me like my mother when I was younger... but covering my mouth so I can't make a noise. As I look round there's more, guns aimed at my head... What's happening? One of the men uncovers their face... Dad?...

THOMAS BASSETT (14)
St Edmund Arrowsmith Catholic High School, Wigan

GHOST TOWN

The Walkers were a normal family. Daniel and his sister Sophie were both ten and had just moved from Metroburg to Hiddenville. 'Wow!' said Daniel, looking around and went upstairs, though he felt a bit suspicious. At 8:30, Daniel and Sophie went to bed. By 11:30, Mum and Dad were asleep too. Late at night Daniel woke up to see a white figure pass him and he started to cry. Sophie turned the light on. Five ghosts were walking around their room. 'Mum! Dad!' the kids screamed, but too late. When they walked in Daniel and Sophie were unconscious.

PATRICK HARRISON (11)
St Edmund Arrowsmith Catholic High School, Wigan

NIGHTMARE REALITY

I quickly scrambled up the decrepit staircase; the heavy footsteps followed close behind me. In what seemed like a lifetime I reached the top, all around me the sky like a black blanket somehow comforting, yet extremely intimidating. I looked down from above to see the busy world below as though it was a child's playset. It was then it hit me, this was it; my life was on the line. His warm eerie breath sent chills down my spine, his bony fingers clung onto my shoulder; a slight shove. I was falling... and that's all I remember.

JESSICA LOUISE LEWIS (14)

St Edmund Arrowsmith Catholic High School, Wigan

THE ICE CREAM MAN

Skeletal trees hung over the extensive path like puppets. The bright moon shone like a lightbulb as I sprinted to my estate. Finally, I reached the end of the path, I was safe... or was I? As I stumbled to the pavement I noticed that everything was different, the houses looked dilapidated and abandoned. It was then I saw a bright pink ice cream van pull up, playing a distorted version of 'Mary Had a Little Lamb'. A dark figure sat in the front seat, we made eye contact and then everything went black.

JOSEPH O'CONNOR (12)

St Edmund Arrowsmith Catholic High School, Wigan

THE UNDEAD GIRL, BACK FROM THE GRAVE

It's beginning to get dark, the dead trees whisper tales of trespassers who dare to walk where I am. All I can hear is the gentle crunch of fallen leaves, discoloured and lacking in moisture - a sign of winter. Moss drips from the sickly dark trees like decayed flesh. I run a little further, I turn and look into the voids that are her eyes, they are murky and defunct, almost like there is nothing there. People say that the eyes are the windows to the soul, but I can tell that hers left long ago.

OLIVIA MARY PATTISON (14)
St Edmund Arrowsmith Catholic High School, Wigan

THE GHOST HOUSE

Ryan slowly crept down the gloomy hallway. As his delicate foot lightly touched the desolate floor an eerie screech filled the deserted, abandoned house. He heard a screech. Not long after he heard the quiet whisper of a creaky, old-sounding voice. 'I can see you, Ryan...' His heart skipped a beat. 'See you later.' The boy trembled to the end of the hallway. There was a corner, a corner he didn't want to turn.
Ryan hesitated for a while until a voice explained. 'It's safe.' Ryan slowly turned round and saw his friend dead. Then he saw the figure...

ETHAN LEWIS DICKSON (11)
St Edmund Arrowsmith Catholic High School, Wigan

THE MYSTERIOUS FORTRESS

It was too late, the door had slammed! Locked! The petrifying scene that greeted me was... a pale bony hand. It felt icy. The hand clutched the old, rotting wood. The wood covered up the rest of the figure. At this sight I felt alarmed! The dark room was filled with hundreds of wooden planks (one of which the figure behind!) On the ground, in the middle of this cramped, wasted space, was a small channel of moonlight flooding across the floor. I had to try to find where it was coming from, I had to try to escape...

EMILY GRIMSHAW-BROWN

St Edmund Arrowsmith Catholic High School, Wigan

THE HORROR WITHIN WESTWOOD MANOR

There it was, mocking them, watching over Westwood village, Westwood manor. Little Jimmy and Tim were playing hide-and-seek; Tim was hiding while Jimmy was looking for him. He saw the manor and quickly remembered what his parents told him about it. Still, he couldn't resist. Its size, its old, deformed look only pulled him closer until he realised that his had was on the doorknob. 'Jimmy!' Tim shouted, 'we can play in here!' All was too late when the door closed behind them and they screamed in fear.
Their parents later saw an article reading: 'Lost Kids'.

THOMAS AINSWORTH

St Edmund Arrowsmith Catholic High School, Wigan

IT'S ALL IN YOUR HEAD

The light bled through my eyelids as I was looking at the haggard chandelier. My dilapidated body struggled to breathe. Eventually I was standing looking at a cracked mirror, I stared at myself up and down. I noticed my hair was messy and my leg was bleeding through my ripped jeans. Suddenly, a dark figure crept up behind me, his face was set in a grimace, and he was gimlet-eyed and had a hunchback. The figure whispered in my ear, 'Wake up!' Then I moved, the murderer was stood there with a knife in his dirty hands...

MOLLY ELIZABETH POTTAGE (14)

St Edmund Arrowsmith Catholic High School, Wigan

THE MANOR

'Uhh, stupid dare!' I mumble, looking at the ancient and supposedly haunted manor.
'Aww, is Jesse scared?' my big brother Matt replies as he sprints into the manor."
'Matt, come out! We don't know what could be in there!' I shout.
'Come on, don't be such a chicke...' Matt replies but is cut off by an ear-piercing shriek.
As I slowly open the creaky, old door, I look around the room, trying to locate my brother. As I turn to leave I feel someone's ice-cold breath on the back of my neck. 'Matt...'

ALISON TRAVIS (11)

St Edmund Arrowsmith Catholic High School, Wigan

THE FINAL STRIKE OF THE KILLER...

I briskly stepped past the murder scene. It was a blur. The moon glistened as it lit up the dismal stratosphere like a torch light reflected onto the dead body! I was interrupted and stationary...
I could only think of the exploitation that this body went through, as that criminal pierced them with the stiletto. The corpse was disfigured (for as much as I could see of it!)
I stuttered away, only to smell the cruel, cunning air that mocked me. It engulfed the body like a blanket. I heard many footsteps, closer, louder and all I remember was *slice...*

MEGAN ELIZABETH HARRISON (14)
St Edmund Arrowsmith Catholic High School, Wigan

THE WOODS

'Come and play.'
'Who's that?' said Billy
As he opened his eyes he saw a figure in the corner of his room. When he stared it vanished into thin, black smoke which led out of his window and over his back fence. He climbed out of his window and towards his fence. It was black and charred as if burned, but there were no flames. As he peered through a small hole he saw the truth: a dark figure, floating, with a purple cloak and glowing red eyes. He then felt a cold hand on his neck...

JACK CLARK
St Edmund Arrowsmith Catholic High School, Wigan

Un-Easy Street

The street reminded me of a horror movie: dangerous, disturbing and dark. Smoke drifted through the air bringing a malevolent presence and bitterness so strong you could taste fear. A horse and carriage awaited on the cobbles, grunting and scraping their hooves, like nails being viciously dragged down a chalkboard, on the dimly lit lane. The midnight clouds tried to hide the moonlight like they were angels of death; trying to block out the light of God's pathway. It created butterflies in my stomach; my knees buckled, sweat dripped down my body. I feared walking the streets...

Gracie O'Gorman (13)
St Edmund Arrowsmith Catholic High School, Wigan

Where Are You?

As I walked into the dark, gloomy house, I was petrified. I slowly crept forward, shaking so much. I so wish I had someone with me right now. I carried on down the long, dark corridor. This was getting scarier and scarier. 'Dion? Dion? Is that you? Dion?' No voice was heard. She'd disappeared! Where could she have gone? There were no doors, windows or stairs. 'Dion?' I swear I just saw her again. *What is happening to me? I'll carry on and see if I can see her. This is getting scarier and scarier.*
'You can't run away now.'

Abbie Lundy (12)
St Edmund Arrowsmith Catholic High School, Wigan

THEY CAN'T HEAR YOU...

Bob entered the graveyard and crept into the dark, gloomy house. Dark as an alleyway, he ran for the spiralling staircase, as it was the only visible thing in his path. 'I regret doing this man!' was heard from miles around with help from the deafening echo. Slamming the door behind, a creepy scene faced him; a bloody rope hanging from the glistening chandelier, with a hand popping out of the grey, tacky wall. 999 was dialled. Down the staircase into darkness, he ran into a corner...
'They can't hear you!' he heard, coming from the phone...

DANIEL CARR (14)

St Edmund Arrowsmith Catholic High School, Wigan

SO CLOSE YET SO FAR...

I can't stand the sight of this prison anymore. It feels as if every step is a climb; every flight a marathon, every second... an eternity. The barred windows cast a depressing light upon the stairs (despite the little light migrating through the cracks). The rusted handle bars on the sides of the steps crumbles as I walk by. This is the hospital that my mother took me to when I was young, the doctors kept telling me I was on my way to overcoming my illness but when I wake up I see this staircase... the never-ending one.

CALLUM PIKE (14)

St Edmund Arrowsmith Catholic High School, Wigan

CAUTION IN THE CASTLE

The moment I entered that ancient castle I knew it was a mistake. However, curiosity got the better of me and I cautiously stepped further into this dark, worrying and terrifying place. The castle seemed abandoned, however a growing fear inside me led me to believe I was not alone. I stumbled up to a spiralling staircase that towered over me like a skyscraper. Every step thundered with the deafening echo. Then I saw a door! As I entered it slammed behind me. Then a large shadow formed behind me with a knife. Then, suddenly, everything went dark.

BEN CLARK
St Edmund Arrowsmith Catholic High School, Wigan

THE CHIMNEY

The chimney smoked cold air on an empty stomach. It supposedly fed off the death that passed through the faded entrance. The window frames ached from years of weathering and lack of much-needed attention. The intimidation of the ancient house caused disarray in my mind, the fog spread contagiously until I couldn't see clearly through my own eyes. Four raw fingers faintly took a hold of my trembling hand. The absence of human nature in the frosty hand sent sharp shivers down my spine. I was walked to the house. The doors swung open. There it was. The chimney...

ETHAN CALVERT (13)

Taverham Hall School, Norwich

NIGHTMARES

David woke up in a cold sweat, as he had for the previous week. It was the same dream, nightmare, that he'd had a hundred times before. A hooded figure. A flash of steel, then he woke up. As usual. He longed not to dream. But he always did. Tonight was different. The dream lasted longer. He watched as the figure stepped over the person he always killed. He looked up. 'You're next!' it whispered menacingly. His last sight was a flash of steel, and a hidden face. Hidden by a hood. Then he felt a burst of pain. Gone.

BEN READ (12)

Taverham Hall School, Norwich

The Awakening

As I open the old decrepit door to the abandoned house near the end of our cul-de-sac, the hinges crack. Pieces of wood splinter off. I take my first peek, I see the wooden stairs completely covered in moss; broken. As I make my way down to the cellar I hear objects being shuffled. I scratch my face and cut my lip, I see this pale girl come towards me so I run past the old stairs and through the decrepit old door as fast as I can. I will never go back to that treacherous house ever again.

Jack William Barnes (12)

Taverham Hall School, Norwich

House 21

Does curiosity ever get the better of you? Well today it got me. I'd always heard rumours about 'House 21'. I'd never listened to them until my brother Tommy disappeared. People say they saw him near 'House 21'.
'He has to be in there!' I cried.
'What if he's not?' replied my friend, Selena. 'What if we get stuck in there?' Selena added. All these what ifs just made me more curious.
We made our way towards 'House 21'. My body shook uncontrollably. My hand touched the icy doorknob. I didn't want to do it but my hand couldn't resist...

Tilly Mordaunt (12)

Taverham Hall School, Norwich

CAUGHT

'Quiet!' I whispered, 'you're going to get us caught.' We were hiding in a garbage disposal, down the back alleys of Manhattan. We were on the run from the RGP (re-generation program). They were after us. It was a calm night, so deserted; we heard nothing, nothing until, *boom!* Someone was on our tail, but we didn't know who. We heard a sinister patter of footsteps coming closer and closer. The streetlights fused, we were in pitch-black darkness. We climbed out of the bin, my friend wasn't there. I felt something cold and sharp on my neck.
'Caught!'

OLIVER JAMES MOORE (12)
Taverham Hall School, Norwich

THE SCREAM

I could hear the scream getting closer. Pulling my body towards it, I saw it. The doll. Watching. Waiting. For my desperate thoughts trying to find the way through the maze, trying to find the perfect route. It moved. I swear it did. 'Mum!' I shouted. No answer. She always answered. I looked back at the doll, dreading what I would see next. Gone. Voices rang in my ears like the Grim Reaper coming towards me. A scream came from downstairs. I could imagine the plastic at the face. Watching. Following. Killing. My mum was gone.
'You're next.'

BEN GRANVILLE (12)
Taverham Hall School, Norwich

A PRESENCE

My eyes couldn't adjust to the sudden darkness surrounding me. The adrenaline was racing around inside. The noises I could hear were disturbing. My paranoia was leading me somewhere else. I was in a mental hospital, in the pitch-darkness. There was a presence, somewhere in front of me. Something watching me. The aura in the room was growing stronger. I knew someone was near. I was holding my breath and making sure I wasn't creating any sudden movements. The fear was worse than all the horror I'd experienced. I felt a hand on my shoulder. It was him.

MADDY LEWIS (12)
Taverham Hall School, Norwich

BRIGHT DARKNESS

The sun shone gold onto the peaceful harbour, the water flashed silver into his eyes. The calm of the harbour sent a chill down his back. His legs ached. He needed sleep. That was why he came here. He staggered back to the hotel. It took him a good 20 minutes but the sunset was worth it. He stumbled through the gate. It screeched slowly. The sun vanished. His legs were dying. Only a few more steps. A cold hand slipped by his neck. 'You shouldn't have come...' and, with a flick of the hand he slumped to the heavens.

WILL WOODHEAD (13)
Taverham Hall School, Norwich

WHAT AM I?

The horror strikes me down like a ton of bricks. I try and get away from the pain but it will haunt me forever. The fear flashes before my eyes, the room is becoming smaller and the people are growing bigger. I feel faint like I am close to death. Memories are flooding back, things I didn't know but now I do. I can remember what happened to me. Why do I feel like this? How's this happening to me? I am craving something. A girl walks into the bathroom; I drain the blood from her body. What am I?

CARYS GREEN (12)
Taverham Hall School, Norwich

THE CAVE

There it was. The cave. People had spoken of this. I began to walk, not wanting to but my feet pulled me forward. I entered the dark abyss, but regretted it. I continued walking until, suddenly, I saw a small, long shape on the ground in front. I began to walk towards it. As I got closer I realised what it was. A human arm. I turned to run but for some reason there was no longer any light coming from the entrance. I then heard a deep, dangerous growl from behind, I dared not look. Then it grabbed me.

BENEDICT WRIGHT (12)
Taverham Hall School, Norwich

Your Worst Nightmare

It's dark, the musty stench creeps towards Jack's nose. Jack walks with trepidation into the church. It was here, the thing from his dream. 'Hello,' whispers Jack. 'I know you're here,' Jack says with false confidence. The lights flicker on. Jack jumps a little but keeps his cool. *Crash!* The old stained-glass window violently drops and shatters into a thousand pieces. Jack quivers just to see a quick glimpse of its shadow.

'Jack...' the noise echoes off the stone walls belonging to the church.

'Y-y-yes?' replies Jack with fright.

'I know what you did, I know what happened...'

Samuel Davies (12)

Taverham Hall School, Norwich

Claw

There in the distance, I caught a glimpse of a strange figure darting through the woods. It was moving towards me. The nearer it came, the more uncomfortable I felt. My legs motioned away but it was creeping closer. Closer. It was out to get me, following my every step. It was an arm's length away. I turned to look at it. Its face was shadowed by trees but the hand was a metal claw and it grew nearer to my face. Nearer with every heartbeat. *Boom, boom, boom!*

Alice Elizabeth Moore (13)

Taverham Hall School, Norwich

TRAPPED

I opened my eyes, sweating and gasping for breath. Looking around I saw nothing, felt nothing but that was what frightened me. My body was weak so I crawled along the cold, hard floor. I scraped my fingernails across it, the sound echoed around the cell-like room. Feeling the walls I realised there were no doors, no windows and no way out. I let my head crash to the ground. Blood came gushing out, dripping onto the floor, running like rivers. Then I wept, not because of the pain but because I knew that I was trapped.

ISABEL CUTTS (11)
Taverham Hall School, Norwich

FLOORBOARDS

What was I doing? The sky shattered the air and I crept through the antique door. It was a distraught building with millions of shards of glass. The door groaned in pain as the hinges creaked. The feathery dust shone like glitter with the light glistening from it. My eyes were pulled towards the silhouette of a distorted figure. I wandered closer, closer. I looked beneath the figure to see dried blood splattered across two creaking floorboards. They started to wriggle and dislocate. I began to hear a scream, the sound of a five-year-old girl. Then silence.

LOUIS HART (13)
Taverham Hall School, Norwich

THE STORM

As I sauntered through the deserted farmhouse, the storm outside grew bigger and bigger, scarier and scarier. I made it through to what seemed like the front hall. A room full of old black and white stained photographs of a couple at a wedding, smiling, looking happy. But not now. Then, suddenly, like a bullet shooting someone, the sky outside turned a mysterious dark colour and the wind started to howl. Then a noise, a noise like death. But then I felt a rush of air pass by me. Then a noise behind me, I knew someone was watching.

RUBY VAUGHAN-JONES (11)
Taverham Hall School, Norwich

MUTANT MOTHER

Mummy shot Beth. It was all over. Daddy had left on a business trip and he wouldn't be back until next week. Mummy's mobile phone was on the table, but I couldn't reach it. All I could do was hide. I had been here for hours, in the attic. I soon heard Mummy come upstairs for her bedtime. I woke up. I must have fallen asleep last night when I was hiding. I crept downstairs and I saw my innocent sister's corpse lying silently on the ground. I didn't know what to do or anything. Then it happened...

JAMES DUFFY (13)
Taverham Hall School, Norwich

Moonlit Wood

In a moonlit wood there stood a withered old tree with twisted limbs. I crept alone, completely oblivious about what would horrify me later. A pungent smell filled the dead, lonely forest. The trees whispered but they didn't articulate enough for me to hear. I squinted through the mist rising from the earthy floor. I saw a terrifying figure dressed in black, wearing a mask that looked like a skull, or was it a mask? I stopped in my tracks. 'Hello? I'm lost, can you help me?' The figure edged towards me, then broke into a sprint. I ran.

Callum Richardson (12)

Taverham Hall School, Norwich

Reflection

I'm lost. I've been looking for hours. I'm about to give up when I hear my mother's voice, 'Charlie!' I follow the warming voice. 'Charlie!'
I follow then it stops. Ahead of me sits a building that looks familiar. I push the door with all my strength. It opens. 'Mum?' Lightning strikes and in the light I catch a glimpse of her face. I run towards it but my face hits a skeleton. I remember now. This is my house. I stroll around looking at the photos. At the end of the corridor there's a huge mirror. There's no reflection.

Joshua A Field (12)

Taverham Hall School, Norwich

UNTITLED

Suddenly, the door opened, instinctively I turned the lights off. It was them, they were coming for me. As quietly as possible I crouched down and bit my lip to stop my breath giving me away. They were coming. When I couldn't hear them I could feel them, closing in like a tiger stalking their prey. I needed to make a move, no time to plan or even start to think what I was doing. So I ran for the door but my legs stopped moving and my cover was blown. They had me this time, there was no escape.

JAMES BURRAGE (12)
Taverham Hall School, Norwich

HORNS

I'm running. All I know is that I'm running. From what? I don't know. But I'm sure it's out to get me. My head whips round as I look over my shoulder and I see a shadow, a menacing shadow full of malice, of something that has one order implanted in its miniscule brain: kill. *Whatever this thing is,* I think, terrified, *it's not human.* I know this because it has two ugly horns protruding from its forehead. I crash through the trees and press myself against the trunk of one. Suddenly, scraping above my head. Then, *slash!* Blackout.

CLARA HOLMES (13)
Taverham Hall School, Norwich

THE RUINS

As I wandered through the ruins there was suddenly an awful smell. I walked up some steps and looked down into a ditch to see the body of a young boy lying there in a pool of blood. I heard a faint sobbing. I looked over to my right. There was a woman on her knees at the top of the ditch. As I watched, a sword was placed at her neck and pulled back. Her eyes widened, then she flopped into the pit. I didn't see the killer. I turned and ran. Then I fell and everything went white...

HUGO DODD (12)

Taverham Hall School, Norwich

DROWNING

I only need two more. I syphon through the mud, finding the small shells. 'Come back in,' the others screech. The fog is coming towards me. Advancing waves are lapping at my feet. I pick up my small bucket and rake, I run through the sandy mud. Never outrun the sea. Fog envelops me. I'm screaming for help but I'm unable to reach shore. The fatal trip. Water sloshes around me, I cannot get up. This is the end. My family need these cockles. I hope the tide takes them in.

EMILY ELIZABETH RINGER (12)

Taverham Hall School, Norwich

THE CABIN

Through the dark misty forest I go, along the twisting track. Disfigured shapes looming over my head. Dry pine needles crackling underfoot, twigs crack behind me. I twirl, confused, scanning the treeline. I carry on trudging towards the cabin. A branch falls to the ground with a soft thud as the eerie laugh echoes amongst the trees. The cabin's porch creaks and as I step through the door a white face appears in front of me and long arms reach out to cover my eyes. I frantically grope for the door but my gaze blackens out slowly as I fall...

GUY HALL (11)
Taverham Hall School, Norwich

AM I DEAD?

It was a cold, dark night, as the trees clawed their long razor-sharp nails at my hotel window. All was deadly silent until, from the corner of my eye, I seemed to spot an unwanted figure. Who was it? Suddenly, the television turned off, so did the light. I felt a cold breath slither down my spine. I heard footsteps, they got sharper and louder until something whispered, 'You're not alone.' That was when the door slammed. I sprinted out of the room, I peered over at the bedroom, my body was lying there smothered in crimson blood...

HOLLY TURNER (13)
Taverham Hall School, Norwich

Untitled

I crept through the forest, the crispy leaves shattered under my toes. The dead trees hung down, catching on my hair. The air hung still and the darkness, cold. I peered round a tree, I heard a noise, breathing. I jumped, a man, he turned to face me. He looked at me with white eyes, no pupils. I froze. He was gone. I blinked, amazed. Suddenly, they were all around me, the man had duplicated, there was fifty of them closing in with wide, white eyes. I quickly hugged the tree. *Climb,* I thought. There was a scream, not mine.

Sam Crossley (12)

Taverham Hall School, Norwich

Underneath

Ghosts. Monsters. Phantom hosts. All the things you're afraid of when you're climbing into bed at night. The things Mum and Dad say aren't real. They're lying. They don't want to worry you, scare you. They want to reassure you but all they're doing is helping themselves. They're wrong. These monsters are real, all of them, but the worst one is right next to you. Lurking under your bed. No one's ever seen one. No one except the children.
I feel it breathing, hear its silence. Something has my leg. I can't move, can't scream as it pulls me underneath...

Molly George (11)

Taverham Hall School, Norwich

WHISPERINGS

It was the 21st December 2004, when on a cold and foggy evening, I cycled through the dense, dark and creepy forest, that lay close to the old abandoned town. Minding my own business I suddenly heard whispering voices in the shadows of the dark night. I stopped and strained to listen to what the voices were saying and more importantly where they were coming from, when I realised the eerie whisperings were calling my name... 'James, James!'
I froze on the spot, aware that the whisperings were growing louder and closer and still I remained unable to move...

ALFIE EDWARD COOP (11)

Taverham Hall School, Norwich

THE TEST

2:13am. It is a late nightshift. Scientists are busy testing an invention made in a lab. The invention is in an oily musty room. A scientist named Tim is in the blingy control room, with his eyes fixated on the 'power-on' switch. With confirmation he rapidly flicks the switch. The machine clicks and finally whirs into life. 2:15am. It seems like a ghostly figure is somehow emerging through the stone walls. It seems to hold a dagger. It is slowly moving towards the invention, but is resisting. The ghost suddenly pushes itself towards the scientists. End of record.

JAMES LIVESEY (12)

Taverham Hall School, Norwich

THE TUNNEL

Summer walks in the park, the call, 'I'll be back by five I promise.' The birds, singing their songs as we walk along, the grass that's as hard as rock. Peace, no clue you're in the town. Then I see it, as quick as a flash. The tunnel! The tunnel that no one dares to enter, the tunnel where girls get attacked. I look at Ellie, uncertainty on my face. 'Go on,' she says, 'I'll follow.' We enter. Reach the first corner... clear. We keep walking and then, bright lights and the hand...

VICTORIA ISHERWOOD (13)

The Streetly Academy, Sutton Coldfield

HOSPITAL FOR SOULS

It is my third night here at the hospital, but already it feels like forever. I wander through the halls, half-conscious, like I'm sleepwalking. But, suddenly, I hear a cry from round the corner. I go to find the source, and what I find is a little girl, slightly younger than me. She is taller though, no, it just looks like that because her feet are floating just above the floor. Then more come. After a few moments, there are ten ghosts surrounding me. If you're reading this, please save me from the ones that haunt me, every night.

EMILY WITCOMB (14)

The Streetly Academy, Sutton Coldfield

A Hike To Remember

I was taking a hike through the Kilohana Square Rainforest, I could hear everything from the leaves crunching under my feet to the birds calling from miles away, but then suddenly there was nothing. When I awoke I was in a cold room with the only light coming in from a gap in the doorway. As I stood up my head began to pound, as I rubbed the back of it I could feel there was blood, a lot of it. I made my way over to the door and opened it, the blinding light flooded in...
'Ah, you're awake!'

Jodie King (14)
The Streetly Academy, Sutton Coldfield

Miley

Laughing, joking. Girls' sleepovers are a part of growing up that every little girl does. A time when doll-playing princesses turn into young adults. Your childish innocence fading into your long term memory. Dolls making their way to the back of the cupboard and make-up going to the front. Eerie sounds fill the room. Miley coming one step, Miley coming two step. Lights flicker only leaving. Thick, white spiderwebs flow across the room, shimmering in the candlelight and a lone live victim struggles against the intricate design that swings gently in the wind.

Charlotte Abby Morgan (14)
The Streetly Academy, Sutton Coldfield

AND THERE HE WAS...

As I trembled, I realised I'd lost my phone. As I turned back, I heard leaves rustling... I then returned to the bunker I was previously in. My phone was gone, so here I was in the middle of nowhere, with no form of communication, or even help. But then... more leaves flew past, and a man appeared in front of me, dressed in blue overalls, a checked claret shirt, leather gloves, a white hockey mask along with a machete. This was it for me, there he was, as well as my final breath of air.

GEORGE CHANCELLOR (14)
The Streetly Academy, Sutton Coldfield

THE MIST

She was getting anxious and her face turned a pale white; the rose shade of her cheeks was a distant memory. Her blood became ice-cold, causing a sudden sickness and violent churning in her stomach. The winds of the forbidding night were calling out to her, but she could hear nothing, nothing other than the thoughts in her head. The girl, standing isolated amongst an army of towering trees, realised her life was becoming evanescent. There was an unbearable mist seeping into her body, imprisoning her. She became empty; her heart trapped in a lifeless cage, deprived of sensation.

COURTNEY WELLS (14)
The Streetly Academy, Sutton Coldfield

No Entry

She ran past the 'No Entry' sign. Unwillingly, Annie followed; she always did. It wasn't finished yet, the fencing wasn't up, the boarding was only half down. The winter sky was a widow's sky - bedarkened and weeping. They jumped over the gaps between the boards, laughing, getting closer to the edge of the pier. She screamed. Clinging onto the side, she grasped the wooden boards, her fingers slowly slipping. That night, she was devoured by the tempestuous sea... Annie, in their bedroom, heard the tapping. Not from the door. From the mirror again. Annie followed, just like she always did.

Rachel Wellman (13)

The Streetly Academy, Sutton Coldfield

The Fear Of The Unknown

The fear of the unknown is the greatest fear of all. Fear, a distressing emotion aroused by impending danger. Unknown not within the range of one's knowledge, experience, or understanding what we can call unfamiliar. We all fear it. Darkness. Death. The end. With the end comes death and with death comes darkness. One day you are full of happiness next you glimpse darkness, an inescapable darkness. The darkness is out there, you can try and scramble away but it will catch up, like the night sky captures the sun.

Beatrice Emily Adams (14)

The Streetly Academy, Sutton Coldfield

MIRROR, MIRROR ON THE WALL

I was woken from my slumber by the knocking. It was 12:07, it came from the mirror. I went to the mirror. I looked in and found a girl staring back at me, her eyes red like the blood that was smeared on her dress. 'Help, I am trapped. You can help me. I have to trade with someone, look.'
In the corner was a girl, I fed her to the mirror. The mirror shattered. There was no twin left just a body and two words: 'Your fault'.
I woke up. It was 12:06 and I heard knocking...

SKYE-ELLIE THOMPSON (13)
The Streetly Academy, Sutton Coldfield

MIDNIGHT GAMES

'It's dark, what are we going to do there?'
'We could play a game of hide-and-seek, it's such a good game!'
As we approached the park I began to shake as the cold breeze crawled up my skin. The park looked dilapidated. The ramshackle swings swung violently. 'Are you sure... you're it!' they chorused, running in opposite directions.
I shouted, 'Guys, where are you?'
30 minutes later... 'Hannah should've found us by now,' said Ryan.
'I know, we have to get her now!'
Painted on the wall in bloodstains read: *You're next!*
'Help!' they screamed.

DARCAI ANDAM-BAILEY (14)
The Streetly Academy, Sutton Coldfield

IT'S IN THE WATER

The raindrops pattered against the car windows riotously. They were parked outside a towering, faceless building. 'You don't have to go in there now,' whispered his driver.

The door creaked open slowly, the moonlight flooded in, showering the furniture inside. He examined the room, turning on a flashlight. Water leaked through the roof, splashing onto the floor, a shadow crept from its contents onto the wall. He enquired closer but something struck him hard in the back of his neck; he fell to the floor, blood seeping across the floor.

RHYS CARTER (13)
The Streetly Academy, Sutton Coldfield

THE RED BALLOON

I nearly drove past her, head down, black coat. Until I saw it, the red balloon. She asked for a lift to a nearby town, holding her balloon string tightly all the way. I stopped at her destination, got out the car and opened her door. A red balloon was left in the car with a scrappy note attached: 'Look in the mirror, Jenny'.

I glared into the mirror with my bloodshot eyes and pale skin. I smiled to myself, thinking a high school prank fooled me. Then I saw my teeth. 'A vampire,' I whispered into the night air...

NIAMH POWERS (14)
The Streetly Academy, Sutton Coldfield

DÉJÀ VU

She couldn't breathe. A gnarling orange grin wiped the smirk off Charlie's face. At each step pain amplified. Blackened bodies and charred bones grasped at her feet. They lay like dolls. Who was once their possessor? No thinking, only running! Too late; she was down. The pain had an unpleasant warmth to it; familiar. A bullet would be mercy. Regrettably she saw the inevitable. An unhindered face... An answer was granted to her question, no matter how forsaken. Thoughts accelerated. Gasped breaths. She was consciously dying, nothing she could do. 'See you soon,' she spoke, gazing at her own lifeless eyes.

CHLOE MURPHY (14)
The Streetly Academy, Sutton Coldfield

THE ROSE

The shattered stone-cold pieces rested against his wizened skin as he lay and reminisced over their memories that once existed. Every day he would shadow over her body, placing a rose to exemplify that something might grow old and die, but if you are there to replace the segments, nothing ever dies. 'I knew you would come back.' A hand rested on his shoulder, his body shivered with a sudden scare.

CHLOE MARIE EVANS (13)
The Streetly Academy, Sutton Coldfield

THE CABIN

'No, no Terry, it's fine,' he had explained, 'there's nothing to worry about.' I can still relive the final moments in the cabin through my mind... where the coffee table stood, the placement of each chair, hell, even the portraits which plastered every mahogany wall. It was a night filled with laughter, joy... and unexpected tensions. Ruby seeped into the logs and surrounding paintings and I, like any other in that situation, knew things weren't just 'fine'. I plunged myself into the white isolation, taking chances with the chill rather than the end of a knife. Death was beckoning.

JACOB NORDSTROM (14)
The Streetly Academy, Sutton Coldfield

THE HAND...

George was just an innocent nine-year-old boy on the wrong street. The lights were pale yellow and the road was abandoned, however, little did George know this street was haunted. He heard a noise. He thought nothing of it until he felt a light, bony hand touch his shoulder. A whoosh of cold breath hit his neck. He was not alone.

DANIEL HAWKINS (13)
The Streetly Academy, Sutton Coldfield

BONES ON FIRE

As I woke up, a stinging filled my insides. My bones felt like they were on fire. Itching, burning. I started screaming, writhing around on my bed. Little white dots crawling out of my pores, out of my nose, my eyes. They were burrowing out, tearing through my flesh as my screams filled the air. Everyone heard them, no one could help. Then it stopped. I woke up. A stinging filled my insides. My bones felt like they were on fire. Itching, burning...

JACK MILLIGAN (13)
The Streetly Academy, Sutton Coldfield

THE HOUSE AT THE END OF THE STREET

The girl walked down the street to the end of the road. At the end of the street there was a house, it looked terrifying. As she walked up the path, ghostly voices kept whispering to her and as she reached the door the rusty handle turned. It squeaked and then the door slowly opened with the old hinges rattling because her hand was shaking. As she opened the door there was pitch-blackness, she couldn't see a thing, all she could see were tiny little feet standing but then the door closed suddenly and she was never seen again.

MIA BEASLEY (13)
The Streetly Academy, Sutton Coldfield

THE CHANGE OF THE CORRIDOR

I walked down the corridor, something cold brushed against my skin. At the bottom of the hall was a cyclone of darkness. Blood started dripping from doors. Suddenly, something grabbed my neck and shoved me against the wall. Its eyes, burning like a single flame, staring inside you. Fear is the only thing I remember. From the outside it was just a delicate creature. Until piece by piece, skin flew off to reveal a monster hidden within. I fell to the ground slamming my head. My eyes opened. The light blinded my eyes. I had become a distant person.

RHIANNON TRAVERS (13)
The Streetly Academy, Sutton Coldfield

A LONG NIGHT

The boy sat up, breathing heavily. His bed was soaked with sweat. This happened every night. This time wasn't any different. He laid his head down back on his pillow and attempted to go back to sleep. He was off quickly into a world of dreams. These dreams weren't so great. His head hurt, but there was nothing to stop it. The images would stay in his mind and haunt him forever, only ending the suffering when the time came to wake up. There was one thing different about this night. He wouldn't be waking up.

DANIEL JOSEPH HOLDEN (14)
The Streetly Academy, Sutton Coldfield

A NIGHT WITH HORROR

He ran frantically, never looking back. The trees rustled in the cold harsh wind, the moon providing his only light. His sweat dripped down his exhausted face as he panted desperately for air. In his left hand he held the briefcase and in the other he held a map, an envelope and a ticket. He turned left into the dark alleyway, when suddenly, out of the mist stepped the tall mysterious figure. A sharp blade in one hand and a sharp, frightening smile on his face. The man had nowhere to run.

NATHAN CASEY (13)
The Streetly Academy, Sutton Coldfield

THE MAN WITH NO FACE

There's a man outside. He followed me and my brother home. It's dark. He's been standing there for a while. He's staring directly at me. My brother is sitting with me but he is acting strangely; he hasn't said anything since we got home. I'm scared. The tall man with long arms is standing outside my house. I turn to my brother but he just stares back at me. I turn around to see where the man is. No longer at the end of the drive, he's standing pressed against the window, facing me. But he has no face...

CAVAN SOMERS (13)
The Streetly Academy, Sutton Coldfield

THE HOUSE

My hairs rose like needles digging into my frozen legs, forcing me to scrape slowly into him. His arms welcomed me, locking me in then banishing light and the last slither of hope. His eyes hung with cobweb-weaved curtains with the off-putting red stain rising in the corner. I stepped in, disturbing the carpet of dust it awakened together with the damp lifting itself from the floor of him. Shadows slowly shifted around me, laughing a vile hackle down my ears and then darting into the darkness.
She smiled at me... 'Want to play a game?'

CAITLIN WILLIAMS (14)
The Streetly Academy, Sutton Coldfield

Blood In The Walls

I crept cautiously towards the blood-wrenched sink. The vile, revolting substance burnt my pale nose, like acid. Bloodstained cutlery resting feverishly across the surface of the peculiar liquid. Several bubbles creating a vast appearance, as I was tempted to lean further towards its thick grasp. My fingertips edged further. Suddenly, a scrawny, pale and transparent hand clenched my wrist, sending electronical vibrations along my crooked spine. I squealed urgently! Gazing along the sideboard; I reached for the abandoned knife, before flinching the hand and watching it slither back into the piped walls!

Daniel Green (12)

Trinity Academy Halifax, Halifax

YoungWriters
Est.1991

YOUNG WRITERS
INFORMATION

We hope you have enjoyed reading this book – and
that you will continue to in the coming years.

If you're a young writer who enjoys reading and creative writing, or the
parent of an enthusiastic poet or story writer, do visit our website
www.youngwriters.co.uk. Here you will find free
competitions, workshops and games, as well as
recommended reads, a poetry glossary and our blog.

If you would like to order further copies of this book, or any of our other
titles, then please give us a call or visit **www.youngwriters.co.uk.**

Young Writers
Remus House
Coltsfoot Drive
Peterborough
PE2 9BF
(01733) 890066 / 898110
info@youngwriters.co.uk